# PRAISE FOR THE OCTOPUS, DADU AND ME

"Full of warmth, wonder, heartache and joy —
not to mention fascinating octo-facts!"
*TASHA HARRISON,*
author of *Clementine Florentine*

"A wonderfully heartwarming story about
one girl's love for her Dadu. A touching tale
of dementia, friendship and the wonder of
an octopus told in a brilliantly contemporary
and readable voice."
*EMILY KENNY,* author of
*The Extraordinary Adventures of Alice Tonks*

"A heartwarming tale of changing family
dynamics, friendship and it features
the best octopus in literature — Ian!
What a brilliant debut!"
*MAISIE CHAN,*
author of *Keep Dancing, Lizzie Chu*

uclanpublishing

# THE OCTOPUS,

# DADU

# AND ME

**LUCY ANN UNWIN**

COVER ILLUSTRATION
BY **SELOM SUNU**

INTERIOR ILLUSTRATIONS
BY **LUCY MULLIGAN**

The Octopus, Dadu and Me is a uclanpublishing book

First published in Great Britain in 2023 by
uclanpublishing
University of Central Lancashire
Preston, PR1 2HE, UK

First published in the UK 2023

Text copyright © Lucy Ann Unwin 2023
Cover illustration by Selom Sunu
Interiors illustrated by Lucy Mulligan
Designed by Amy Cooper
Comic book background © Shutterstock, 2023

978-1915235-03-9

1 3 5 7 9 10 8 6 4 2

Set in 11/18pt Museo 100 by Amy Cooper

A CIP catalogue record for this book is available from the British Library.

Printed and bound in Great Britain by Clays Ltd, Elcograf S.p.A.

To my own girls' wonderful grandparents . . .

Maureen and Tony.
Who would have adored them.

Tara and Pete.
Who they utterly adore.

# PART ONE

PART ONE

# CHAPTER 1

An aquarium. Not exactly the best place to be when your world's falling apart. I was wedged on a too-small chair as schools of little kids rushed past me like sharks. Why did Mum and Dad think a trip to see some fish would cheer me up? I was twelve, not two. And this place was dark and echoey and weird.

I wiped my tears on the back of my hand and tried to sniff myself back together. I'd cried so much my skin was raw and puffed right out of my face.

*Puffer fish.*

I'd just passed one of those. I had not been ready for how deep-down strange they looked all un-puffed. Now, I was stranded at this little colouring-in table while the lights flashed from blue to red to green, making my tummy do flips. I needed to move.

Mum and Dad could see me from the cafe area. They were "giving me space", but not a lot of it.

I snuck a glance at them and tried not to imagine being wrapped in a hug. I wanted to nestle in so deep that everything except my own breath disappeared. I wanted it so much I ached. But this was all their fault! I didn't have them now, I didn't have my wonderful Dadu, I was completely alone.

*Look at the fish, Sashi,* I told myself.

I stood up to read the info-card-thing in front of me.

Juvenile, Male.

But before I got a chance to learn about "habitat" and "feeding habits", I glanced into the tank to see two bright and beady eyes looking right at me.

*Oh.*

*Not a fish.*

*Octopus.*

'Hello there,' I whispered, 'Do *you* give hugs?'

He looked back at me, but didn't answer.

Wow, he was gorgeous. Each sucker a perfect circle, his tentacles moving like pencil strokes. I had to draw him, right now. I reached into my back pocket for my ever-ready mini-sketchbook, but he folded himself away as I peered into the tank.

I couldn't blame him. There was a baby crying somewhere; a constant, screeching wail. With the weird light show, the heat and that terrible kid-siren, this was the worst place on earth.

*I'm not like the others, octopus. I won't flash you with photos, or tap on the glass, or storm past hunting for Nemos.*

He edged behind his seaweed shield. Grey goosebumps studded his tentacles, his head-lump-thing swayed in the water and his eyes were still locked on mine.

*Come back out,* I willed.

Then in a sudden flurry, he was there. I burped out a giggle as I pressed myself closer. He spread the glass with his sucker-things, then coiled and spiralled sideways, a bright corally-red. Where were his eyes hid now? *There.* He stared right at me as he retreated, shifting to brown, to coal-black, then grey. Back in his hole.

He looked like he wanted to tell me something.

## CHAPTER 2

### EARLIER THAT DAY . . .

Dadu was yelling at Mum, his face like somebody else's. He didn't mean it. He couldn't help it. But I still couldn't watch.

I tried to edge further away, but I was already up against the wall of his room. I covered my face with my hands. I could still hear Dadu yelling, spitting terrible insults at Mum as if she was the worst person on earth — or he was. I covered my ears instead.

Mum sat straight-up in the plastic-covered chair and wiped her wet cheek. 'It's all right,' she murmured. She took Dadu's hand and started stroking it. 'We're here. We're your family, we're going to look after you. Calm down.'

He shook her off, 'What? Get Away! Off! Now! Stay away from me!'

'It's OK,' said Mum, backing up slightly.

I sank onto my heels.

'It's not OK, Helen,' my dad squeezed her hand and glanced at me, before squatting in front of Dadu's wheelchair. Dadu was still opening and shutting his mouth and gripping and releasing the armrests. "Agitated", Mum called it, when he got like this. I hated it. *Poor Dadu.*

It had never happened until they moved him to this "care home", for old people. He should be in his own house, with his own stuff! That's what Mum and Dad had said before they'd gone and changed their minds.

'Dad – Baba – it's me, Manu. You can't talk to Helen like that, OK?'

Dadu might have been shouting, but his face looked more scared than angry.

'Helen? Manu? What?' He sighed and his eyes wandered right over me and round to the door. 'I need to see my nurse. One of you people fetch her for me, would you? It should be teatime now, and there isn't any.'

My heart froze as he failed to see me. Dadu had stopped recognising us a while back now, but it was still a shock. He had something called "dementia", which basically meant his brain wasn't working properly and he forgot stuff. A lot of stuff. It was the worst. It happens to old people sometimes. Dadu had been pretty old when Dad was born, and he was *really* old now. Plus, he seemed to have aged about a hundred years in the few weeks he'd been living here.

Mum left the room to fetch a carer and then suddenly we were leaving. Mum and Dad stooped to kiss Dadu goodbye, but he turned his face away from them. I just ran out the room and waited in the corridor. Next time he might not be so bad; I would give him a kiss then.

On the way to the car, Mum and Dad walked ahead of me, their heads bent together, murmuring. Mum turned around and smiled, but they still let me trail behind them, alone.

Then, once we were in the car, I found out what they'd been talking about.

Mum started driving, and Dad put his hand on the back of her seat and twisted round to face me.

'Me and your mum have decided it's time to stop visiting Dadu now, Sashi darling.'

*What?* I strained against my seat belt. 'But he's just having a bad day – he's not always like that.'

One day he would see me again, I knew it. He'd pull me onto his lap and ask me how my drawing was going. We just had to be patient.

Mum caught my eye in her mirror. 'We have to accept the way things are, Sashi. I know this is hard, but he's not coming back the way you remember him.'

*Not true!* Bells rang in my ears muffling what they were saying. I flopped back in my seat and Dad patted my knee. I kept hearing them talk of *"letting go of the past"*, even *"saying goodbye"*, but I tried to block it out.

I *wouldn't* "accept" it! I couldn't.

And I hadn't even *said* goodbye to him today.

I started to cry, silently, just like Mum had.

## NOW . . .

Now I locked eyes with the octopus and tried to blink away fresh tears. I pressed my forehead to the glass – this beautiful octopus would just have to put up with me, I didn't want Mum and Dad to see me upset again. I'd lost it in the car. Mum had been talking as though Dadu had died, but he hadn't. They didn't know what they were on about.

As we'd pulled up at our house Dad had declared it was "all too depressing" and suggested we come here to take our mind off things.

'Oh, we haven't been to the aquarium in ages!' Mum had said, as though it were a great idea, when clearly it was terrible. She'd yanked off the handbreak-thing and now, here we were.

The octopus moved to the top of the tank, so I couldn't really see him with the reflections on the glass.

I turned away and pulled out my phone – I needed to talk to someone. I needed to tell Darcie.

I swiped my screen on and tapped out a message.

**ME:** Darcie, you wouldn't believe what Dad's done!

I slumped against some fake stonework and stared at my screen, waiting. My breath calmed down, and I did a huge sniff.

Darcie was my best friend. She was the funniest and smartest person I knew – cleverer than most grown-ups, for real. And she always knew what to do.

*Buzz, buzz.*

*Finally.* I swiped the screen.

**DARCIE:** Uh oh . . . What?

I told her what Mum and Dad had said in the car.

**ME:** Just like that. No warning or anything!!!

Mum had gone on about how Dadu was living in the past; how he thought he was back in Calcutta, in India, where he grew up. I knew all that already. For a while, Dadu had mistook Dad for his brother, which was seriously weird — his brother died years ago. He didn't recognise me or Mum at all. He thought we were complete strangers.

But that didn't mean he wouldn't come back to us. He was still my wonderful Dadu.

**DARCIE:** Oh, Sashi, that's the worst. Where are you? Wanna meet?

**ME:** Man, don't ask! Family trip.

**DARCIE:** Why now? Is he worse?

I couldn't bring myself to type exactly what Dadu had said, but I told Darcie enough to give her the general idea.

**ME:** But he couldn't help it — it's a dementia thing.

**DARCIE:** Your Dad knows that, right? I don't get it.

**ME:** *I guess he thought it was too upsetting for me to see or whatever. Or that Dadu's not himself anymore.*

I hated that phrase: "not himself". It didn't make any sense. He was still Dadu, right? Who else? And he needed our help. How could we just stop visiting him?

**DARCIE:** Virtual hugs, Sash-a-lac, I wish I could do something.

A stream of GIFS followed, then:

**DARCIE.** So where is this family trip anyway? Anything cool there? Good distractions?

**ME:** Aquarium!!!!????!

**ME:** I mean, what's that about?

**DARCIE:** What? Love the aquarium! Well jel!

Ha! I shrugged.

**ME:** Well, there IS a pretty cool octopus . . .

She sent a GIF of a teensy octopus reaching out and touching someone's finger – like a baby, underwater E.T. It was seriously cute. I smiled.

**DARCIE:** Say "hi" to it from me.

**ME:** Er, yeah . . . ? See you Monday. x

I glanced round. So, the lights could be kinda pretty when you got used to them. And *this* strange creature I liked, for sure. He floated in front of me again, graceful as a ghost, rippling through his muddy colours, then gliding back.

'My friend Darcie says "hi",' I whispered.

There was a sign over his tank.

*An octopus has 3 hearts.*

*If an octopus looses an arm, it can re-grow it.*

Good facts.

I could do with an extra heart right now — to forgive Mum and Dad.

I shoved my phone back in my pocket and sighed.

I wished I could just hold Dadu's hand again.

I raised my fingers to the glass of the tank like the hand in the GIF, 'What about you?' I murmured, 'Will you hold my hand?'

And for just the quickest moment, one sucker-covered tentacle grazed the glass behind my fingers.

# CHAPTER 3

The next morning, Mum and Dad were being way too nice. Pancakes? This was not a standard Sunday. But my favourite breakfast changed nothing. Even with golden syrup. There was *no way* I was going to forgive them. Mum leant down and kissed me on the head as she swooshed past to clear up plates, her long, blond hair tickling my nose. I froze, then got back to rolling the perfect lemony pancake mouthful.

'OK, that's it. I am never eating another octopus!' Dad slammed his book down on the table.

*Octopus? What-now?*

My cheeks had gone hot, as though I'd been caught with a guilty secret, but I hadn't.

'How ridiculous!' Mum sighed over the dishwasher, but she was smiling.

'Dad, why are you reading about octopuses all of a sudden?'

He leant towards me, elbows on the table. 'Well, you seemed pretty engrossed with that one at the aquarium yesterday, Sashi, my love, and you know I like to stay abreast of your various obsessions!' He was grinning at me wildly which just made me angry, strangely. Normally, we loved getting stuck into a project together.

But not today.

I stared down at the tentacles I'd been absently sketching in the syrup with my fork.

'So, I popped down the bookshop this morning. Crack of dawn!' He tapped the cover and waited. I could feel his eyes boring into the top of my head. Finally, he gave up and twisted round to face Mum '. . . and I must say – I'm only three chapters in but I'm an octopus convert! Off the menu for me, that's for sure.'

'So, how often have you eaten octopus this year then, Manu?' Mum straightened up, eyebrows raised. 'Scratch that – how often have you eaten octopus *in your life*? Because if you're getting any little ethical twangs, there's always room at the vegan table.'

I stifled a snort. My mum was a vegan, she doesn't eat any animal foods at all – so, no milk, eggs, cheese or lots of other random stuff. She always says dairy farming is killing the planet – and that Dad's tea-drinking was 90% responsible for the world's milk production. She's always trying to persuade him to go veggie at least, so a tiny concession to stop eating something he never eats anyway – definitely not going to be popular.

'Did you know *this* though, Helen?' Dad carried on, 'They can open childproof caps!' He sneaked a wink at me. 'That makes the average octopus more intelligent than Sashi!'

'Oi!' I stood up and shoved him in the shoulder, harder than I'd meant to. My chair toppled over at the same time.

'Sashi!'

My mum's scold made my cheeks flood pink again, but then she smiled at me and I felt even worse.

*Stop pretending you're nice!*

'He's going to start eating *me* next!' I lashed out at Dad again, but he snaked his arm round my waist and pulled me onto his lap.

14

'Listen to this, though,' he said. 'They're not like fish – happy as Larry in their tanks. It says Octopuses *know* they're in captivity! You can tell it from their behaviour. Crikey.'

'Dad, it's an old-person science book.' I was trying to zone him out, but the word "captivity" rang out. Poor octopuses. *Anyway* . . . 'There aren't even any pictures. And I don't want to know how clever fish are when they look at me with their big, sad fish eyes.'

'Ah, look at *your* big, sad fish eyes,' said Dad. He was teasing me; blinking up at me with his own brown eyes wide. He made them look huge and way more sad than mine.

He always called me a fish because my name sounded like "sashimi", the Japanese food. It had started at the sushi restaurant on our road, when I was little. Over the years it'd gone through Sashimi, Fishimi and Fish-dish to Little Fish, although they all made an appearance sometimes.

I quite liked it, but Mum *hated* it. Especially as my name actually has a really beautiful story.

It means "moon" in Sanskrit, and there was a full

moon the night I was born. When Dadu came in to visit me he apparently kept staring out the window and Mum had shouted at him, telling him to "stop gazing at the bloody moon and look at your beautiful granddaughter". He'd looked at me and smiled and muttered "Sashi", and Mum had named me on the spot. Family legend.

But of course my goofball father had to make a joke of it. He'd been through plenty of ridiculous moon-based nick-names too, especially when we'd been reading *The Magic Faraway Tree*. But it was 'Little Fish' that had stuck. Even Dadu had adopted it eventually, and somehow when he said it I *loved* it. Instead of a joke, it felt really special.

'An octopus,' said Mum, 'is not a fish, Sashi. As you know full well. Don't pretend to be less clever than you are.' Mum cleared my plate from the breakfast table. Dad still had me pinned round the waist, ignoring how mad I was at him, and lost in his reading again.

'Manu, you *are* going to get the barbeque food together this morning, aren't you? We're heading out at twelve.'

'Heading where?' I asked. My head was now filling with images of octopuses – octopi? – pretending to be more stupid than they were, just as Mum said I did. Hiding their big brains in their deep-sea-tentacled bodies. It would make a sick comic – I wanted to hole myself up for the entire day and draw it. What would they be thinking and planning in those brains? I needed my sketchbook.

I drew all the time. Dadu had started me off drawing comics when I was little, and I'd never stopped. I'd even had a strip published in a kids' magazine. It was framed above my bed.

'We're meeting Hassan's family on the beach, my love. I thought it would be nice for you to spend some time with your friend. Get out the house.'

'Oh, Mum, seriously? He's not *my* friend, he's *your* friend's kid!'

'Don't be silly, Sashi. What nonsense!'

'You know we've not actually been proper friends since we were about *six*, right?'

Dad snapped out of his reading. 'Whaaaat? You and Hassan are wonderful friends, just like me and his dad. We can all play a bit of beach cricket!'

He squeezed me round the waist.

My dad was an engineer at the Highways Agency – which mainly meant driving up and down the motorway with a stick-on flashing light on the roof. He and Hassan's dad both started work there on the same day, ages ago. "Comrades of adversity", Dad called them – I think that meant they did some war thing together . . . a training day, maybe? Our families have been glued together ever since.

'Hassan's not gonna want to play cricket with you, Dad.' I rolled my eyes.

'What? Why not?' Dad shook his arms out, as if he were warming up for a game right there and then. 'Ah, that boy's the coolest.'

I groaned. Hassan was everything I wasn't. Loved by teachers, leader of the in-crowd, trophy-winning sports captain . . . and now even my dad was being sucked in.

'Y'know he's twelve and you're a grown-up, right? You sound like one of the wannabes at school.'

'Food!' said Mum.

'Eh?' Dad looked puzzled before the memory

dawned, then lifted me from his lap and plopped me on to my feet. 'Looks like I'd better go and skewer some kebabs.'

Time to escape before they had me chopping veggies. My drawing time was going to be way too short. I reached to the shelf and grabbed my pens – I'd better get started.

# CHAPTER 4

Hassan was down by the waves, throwing stones. Still super-tidy, despite the sea wind. How was *that* possible? But Hassan wouldn't be seen dead looking scruffy. He even carried a comb in his pocket. If I drew him, I would definitely add in a little tooth-sparkle when he smiled. *Ping!* *Ugh.*

Did neatness make you cool? I looked down at my hoodie — all crumpled — my tatty converse, the big holes in my leggings and laughed. Definitely doomed.

Anyway, Hassan was way too popular to hang out with me, so *I* wasn't interested in spending all afternoon with him. At all.

If Darcie was here we could fossil hunt. But at least I'd brought my proper sketch book to do more octopus drawings – I was really proud of the one I'd drawn this morning. *Octopus Uprising.* I grinned.

I made my way down to the big rock I always

used to sit on with Dadu. It was wide and curved into a seat shape, smooth to the touch, worn down by years of lapping waves. *Slurp, slurp, slurp.* I always thought of the waves like a big, rough tongue licking away at the beach. Dadu would pat the big rock – "Come park your bottom here, Little Fish". – and I would snuggle into his side; the heat of the rock warming me, the sun on my face, breathing deep on Dadu's ever-present eucalyptus-y scent of Vicks VapoRub. Dadu would just put his arm around me and not say anything. It was the only time I could ever be totally still by the sea; I'd felt no need to throw or collect or clamber like usual, or pull out a book or sketchpad.

Now the rock felt cold. I got out my pencils.

The grown-ups were already laughing and hugging and unpacking all the food; deckchairs up, music playing through a little speaker. Hassan's mum was steadying herself with a hand on Mum's shoulder as she replaced a fallen flip-flop. They glowed with comfort and happiness.

And the food was insane. They'd made kebabs

and chicken, salads and guacamole, boiled corn on the cobs ready to grill and there was some spicy fish thing that smelt amazing. Dad also insisted on bringing his childhood favourite to every outdoor meal – cheese sandwiches stuffed with salt and vinegar crisps. And a big bottle of chilli sauce, of course. There was enough food to feed thirty. They were beach barbeque experts.

'Hassan!'

A cloud of seagulls took off from where they'd been stalking over the rocks.

'Hassan! Look, Sashi's here!' It was his dad. *Great* I tried to disappear into my sketchbook, gulls forming on the page as quickly as they honked and circled overhead.

Hassan picked his way across the beach. His dad leant over and ruffled my hair as they met at my rock.

'Hey,' his son offered, looking bored as he plonked

down beside me and leant over my shoulder to see my seagull picture.

I stood up and stepped away. I didn't want to share Dadu's rock with anyone else.

Hassan's dad grabbed my shoulder and gave it a hearty shake. 'Why do I not see you round our house any more, eh, Sashi?'

'Er—' *Because your son is too cool for me now?*

'Dad, stop it! Sashi doesn't have to come round. She's busy with her proper friends.'

*Gee, thanks for the sarcasm.* I doubted my one actual friend was on his radar.

Hassan tugged at my cuff and darted off, beckoning me to follow. I snatched up my sketchbook, pencils and bag, half dropping them. 'Hey! Hang on a sec.'

'What?' He turned. 'Oh, soz.' He took my things off me and started to pack my bag. *Annoying.* I grabbed it back, shooting fireballs with my eyes, and he flopped on the beach with a sigh.

'Hey, sorry,' he said. 'I couldn't face it. Dad thinks I need help with my friendships!'

'What, is he not a fan of the cool crew?'

'"Cool crew"? *That* sounds horrible.' He puffed out a breath, and his shoulders sank.

'Hassan, what are you on about? You love it. With all those silly boys from the football team. Parading round like you own the school . . .' He was acting almost normal, but I didn't buy it.

'Right. I guess. They're an OK laugh. I just want to play football, really. Who else am I going to hang out with, the Maths club?'

*Er, me?*

I didn't get it. If he wasn't completely into himself, why the comb? I shook my head. 'You love it,' I said.

'Whatever.' He picked up a stone and threw it into the sea in a perfect long arc.

Why was I even having this conversation? I wanted to go back to my drawing. I stood to head back to my rock, but Hassan let out a pathetic groan. I sat back down.

'Ah, soz little Sash, here I am moaning about my life, when I'm supposed to be cheering you up.' He threw his meaty arm around my shoulder, invading my personal space and flooding me with his weird musky body scent.

There was so much wrong with this I didn't know where to start.

Firstly: *little?*

Secondly: *Sash?* — OK, so he used to call me that, when we were about seven, but we were NOT on nickname terms now.

Thirdly: *you've got to be kidding with the arm-invasion?*

But last: *why on earth was he supposed to be cheering me up – has someone asked him to?*

'OK, get your arm off me,' I hissed, shrugging myself out from under its weight. 'And I'm fine, *thanks.*'

Hassan blushed pink and backed away, his hands up in surrender.

'Sashi, I'm sorry, I'm an idiot.' He folded his arms self-consciously. 'I didn't mean to upset you, I'm not very good at this. Your dad thought you could use an old friend, that's all. Because of your Dadu? I'm sorry . . .'

A sob rose to the back of my throat at the mention of Dadu, and a crack of guilt opened up in me – maybe he *had* just been trying to be nice. In his own, awkward way. *Could* I talk to him? Hassan knew Dadu quite well from when we were little.

Dadu would tell us some of his stories from back home, or sit and colour with us. Dadu had been an engineer like Dad, but for him it seemed to mean drawing beautiful pictures of bridges, so *I* think he was more of an artist. He would trace pictures in his beautiful fine lines for me and Hassan to fill, while slipping us creamy sondesh – his favourite Bengali sweets – from a greasy paper box.

But that had been a long time ago. *This* Hassan wouldn't understand.

'What are you two up to?' I jumped. *Mum.* Her hand grazed the middle of my back. She had a magic way of knowing the best moment to show up. 'Have you seen what you're sitting in the middle of?'

*Yer-what?* I shook my head to release the mouth-watering memories of sondesh, and scanned the empty beach around us.

'Er, hi, Helen . . . in the middle of?' Hassan exchanged a look with me and shrugged.

'Sea squirts.'

'Sea . . ? Mum, what are you on about?'

She squatted on a rock and picked up something that looked like a prune.

'Look! They look like your eye-bags after a night playing FIFA, Hassan!'

Hassan's fingers shot to his perfect cheeks. He stared at my mum, wide-eyed, for a full second before he realised he was being teased. Then his face broke out in the kind of grin I hadn't seen on him in a while.

'Actually, it's a marine invertebrate,' Mum chortled.

I picked one up and examined it

Hassan frowned. 'Why are they called—*argh*!'

I'd squeezed the little prune and it squirted Hassan with some sort of gross sea-juice. He jumped back about a metre and Mum nearly fell over laughing.

'What the . . .' Hassan was staring down at the wet stain on his pristine polo shirt. He was going to flip his lid.

I picked up another one, paused for a fraction of a second, then squirted him again – eyes locked on him to see what he'd do. Super slowly he reached down to the beach, scooped up one of his own, then squeezed a jet back at me. I shrieked and dodged it just in time.

We chased each other round the beach squirting

the dried-up little prunes and falling over. We ended up breathless and collapsed on the pebbles.

Hassan turned his head to the side to look at me. 'Y'know, I can't tell you how much I needed that.' He was still laughing and his hair was a total mess. I felt a surge of affection for him – he looked like my old Hassan.

'Me too,' I said. And it was true. I did feel better. It was nice to have my friend back.

'Man, I must look a mess.' He sat up on the beach and whipped his comb out of his jeans pocket, tracing his perfect parting.

I couldn't resist – I reached in my bag for my mobile and snapped a photo of him, then sent it to Darcie:

**ME:** Guess who I'm on the beach with today?

**DARCIE:** WT?!? Is that HASSAN? I want the deets.

**ME:** Can you make a juice bar breakfast special? Tomorrow morning? Lots to tell you.

**DARCIE:** Yup. See you AM. x

★★★

The next morning, I was up and out the house within half an hour. I cut through the park then sped through the lanes on my bike, dodging shopkeepers setting up and slowing to freewheel past all the amazing art sprayed on to the walls: puppies, dragons, robots. How did they manage to get such detail with a spray can? I could only dream of being that good. I stopped dead at a new picture I'd not seen before: a huge, orange octopus peering out of the brickwork, with all its gross brain on show. How were they suddenly everywhere? Was the universe trying to tell me something? I shook my head. *Weird*.

I reached our regular meeting point, skidded my bike to a stop and leant it against the wall, ignoring Dad's voice in my head nagging me to lock it up.

If only I had some sort of plan to help Dadu, everything would be better. And Darcie was my planning partner: 100%. Like when we'd started comic club at school and won a Headteacher's Award. Or when we'd collected all those wild poppy seeds, then made £20 selling them door-to-door. If Darcie thought something was a good idea, it usually was.

At the door of the juice bar, I paused. Walking in here was always a bit of a shock. Everything was painted orange or sunshine-yellow or lime green, and the super-sweet smell hit you the second you

30

stepped in. It felt like it should be tropically warm, but it was actually freezing. Like that feeling when everything around you is happy, but you still feel sad. I shivered and glanced around: Darcie wasn't here yet.

I'd lied to her really, and the guilt sat heavy in my stomach right next to the porridge I'd had for breakfast. My texts yesterday had hinted at gossip about Hassan, but the truth was I just wanted to talk more about Dadu. Not exactly much fun. But my dad had been right; I did need a friend to chat to, he'd just chosen the wrong friend.

The lady behind the counter smiled at me patiently, kid-sized cup and Sharpie in hand, as I gazed at the thousands of choices. *Pine Forest Perk-up, Just Keep the Beet, Brekkie Berry Buzz, De-tox-a-licious.* I just loved the names and imagining what they would all taste like. But where to start? Maybe if there were just four choices, I would try them all but, as it was, I gawped for five minutes then always had the same.

'Blueberry Blitz, kid-sized, please.'

'Of course. Sashi, right?' She wrote my name on the cup. I loved her accent — it was full of extra 's'

sounds and made her sound really kind. That, and the fact she was always actually really kind to us.

'And is your brainy friend on the way? Shall I mix her one up, too?'

'Er . . . yeah, sure.'

*My brainy friend?*

'Sit down. I'll bring them over.'

I went to sit in our usual booth at the back. Did Darcie just give it off in waves? I guess there was a certain confident way she spoke, and walked, and held her head up – not like me. Mum said I scuttled around like a little mouse and was always telling me off for whispering.

But Darcie wasn't like the clever kids who made a big show of not even trying. She worked hard too. This was why we met here before school; to get all the gossip out the way. Darcie would NOT talk during lessons.

When she finally pushed through the door, she was flapping.

'Ah, good timing,' said the juice lady. 'Take your drinks. One for you, one for the little one.'

*Wow, way to rub it in.* Darcie *was* a full head taller than me, but still.

She bundled over to our booth with the smoothies, looking all wrapped up for winter already; a long scarf holding down her blond hair and her blue eyes watery.

'Sorry, sorry, sorry, sorry! I meant to get here earlier, but Mum's going away for a conference so it's a packing frenzy in our house. Hard to escape!'

Darcie lived alone with her mum in this mad seafront apartment. Her mum just happened to be some famous tech person or something. She always had her picture in magazines and had to go away a lot. When she did, Darcie's aunt babysat and Darcie could do pretty much what she wanted – usually extra homework.

Darcie was basically all kinds of awesome, and I had no idea why she hung out with me. I just didn't question it too much and hoped for the best.

'Tell me *everything*,' she flopped down on the bench and shuffled in sideways till we were nose to nose. 'Did he give you a tour of his trophy cabinet? Show you selfies of his six best haircuts?'

I snorted mid-suck, sending bubbles out of my cup.

'Aw, you know what? He's not that bad.'

'Whaaat? Are we talking the same boy here? Mr Cool? Floats round on his own body spray-scented cloud?'

'Well, yes, he *is* a bit in love with himself . . .'

She grinned. 'I thought you didn't like him. Is he your new BFF now?'

'What . . . NO! You know he wouldn't even look at me at school.'

'*Exactly*, Sash-a-lac.'

When we'd started secondary school together, Hassan had instantly had his own group. It was obvious he wouldn't want to hang with me any more so I avoided him as much as possible.

'I just don't want you getting hurt, y'know . . .'

'He was actually really sweet on the beach yesterday. We messed around . . . it was nice!'

'Oh, my heart is melting! So this is what you brought me here to discuss? That Hassan is "really sweet" under all that hair wax?'

She was more interested in Hassan than I thought she'd be, but at least she'd clued on it wasn't the real thing I wanted to talk about.

'Ugh, no, sorry.' *New subject.*

I took a deep drink for berry strength and told Darcie all the details from Saturday morning that hadn't fit in the texts – how Dadu had acted towards my mum, everything my dad had said in the car, how now the plan was suddenly to never see him again. Just like that.

Darcie edged off her bench and on to mine, nudging me gently with her shoulder. For a minute we just sat there. I thought I would cry, but I must have used up all my tears at the aquarium. Then I straightened up. I needed a plan.

'So Darcie, I need to get him remembering again . . .'

'Oh Sashi, I'm not sure.'

'He's been so much worse since he's been in the home. He just needs to be with his family . . . with me.'

'But . . .' Darcie span her cup round on the table. 'He was always going to get worse, over time, wasn't he? Isn't that the trouble?'

'Not if he's with me – I can make him remember! He needs me, I know he does. So listen, I need to do something. What if . . . I signed him out, took him home and settled him in, and then when Mum and

Dad got back, they'd see how happy he was and, and . . .'

Darcie's face was saying "bad plan". And as I'd heard the words out loud, I'd realised it would never happen. I couldn't just break him out and set him free. They would never let a twelve-year-old do that. He couldn't even walk the distance back. Fine. Fine. So, this was where Darcie stepped in with a better plan; a different way to make my parents see sense.

Darcie took hold of my hands and I saw tears in her eyes.

I sank back into the bench.

'Oh, Sashi. It must be so hard to see him like that . . . but, you know your Mum and Dad love him too, right? I'm sure they must have . . . y'know . . . thought it through?'

I whipped my hands out of hers and slammed them on to the bench. 'Thought through leaving him trapped there!? Not seeing him? That makes no sense!' *Not a plan.*

'They're trying to protect you.'

'From *Dadu*?'

'From being sad.'

'Well, they're not doing a very good job about it.'

'No . . .' she said slowly. 'They're not. Look, listen to me – some plans take time to work out OK. You don't need to give up on him . . . but listen, this is what we're going to do . . .'

I sighed and closed my eyes.

'. . . You have to trust your mum and dad . . .'

I groaned, but Darcie took my hands again and it felt good to let her.

'And you . . . yes, you need to find a distraction. You have to not think about your Dadu for a while and get a new focus. It'll do you good, Sashi. I promise.'

I opened my eyes and looked at my friend. This was NOT the plan I'd been hoping for, but I trusted Darcie. So: no thinking about Dadu. Find a distraction.

Except Dadu was all I thought about, and nothing would be able to distract me from him.

# CHAPTER 5

**NEARLY 6 YEARS EARLIER . . .**

A huge, crinkly pile of birthday wrapping surrounded me like a nest; I snuggled in deeper. Everything was perfect. I was seven. Almost a teenager! Dadu was right behind me, with his hand on my shoulder. It had to be him because no one else's hands were hot like that. Seriously, he was so warm. I could feel a wave of heat right down my back.

I span round and jumped into his lap.

'Oof!' he laughed. 'Glad to see seven-year-olds aren't too big for a cuddle!'

'What are you *talking* about, Dadu? I'll never be too big! You'll just have to get stronger!'

'Oh really?' he said, tugging me deeper in and swaying me from side to side. 'Maybe I'll be sitting on *your* lap in a few years' time, and you can rock me and feed me biscuits!'

When he laughed his belly bounced up and down, taking me with it.

My brand-new bike was gleaming in front of us, in the middle of the living room floor. All mine. Lime green with white lightning bolts stencilled on and a huge, shiny, black bell.

'Just look at it!' Dadu said, clearly reading my mind. 'What a magnificent machine!'

I giggled. 'Do you want a go then, Dadu?'

'Do I want a *go*?' He shifted me to one knee. 'Do I ever! You won't catch me once I've got going on that beauty. Greased lightning!' He made a big whoosh with his arm, then chuckled.

*Since when was lightning* greasy? *Silly Dadu.*

My new bike needed to go outside, but then, I also wanted to keep it here on the carpet for ever so it would stay shiny and perfect and new. I'd learnt to ride on a second-hand bike so small Dad said my knees looked like they'd hit my chin! This one looked huge . . . but still too small for Dadu.

Mum started to collect up all the wrapping paper and shove it in a bin bag. *Too soon!*

'I think we're all done, Birthday Girl,' she said.

'Do you want—'

'Er, hang on. Hold your horses.'

Dadu lifted me up and plonked me on the cold seat next to him. I shivered. Then he hooked his hand under the sofa and pulled out a rectangular wrapped gift and a boring-looking brown envelope.

'It's not a bike, Little Fish,' he said, 'but I hope you like it.'

Dadu's presents were hilarious.

'Is it a box of chocolates, Dadu?'

'Sashi!' Mum was telling me off, but Dadu was smiling.

He took back the box. 'Ah, well, maybe I'll eat them all myself then, if you don't want them . . .'

'Noooo!'

Last birthday he'd wrapped up a big bag of Haribo. To be fair, they'd been super delicious. Who doesn't like sweets? If these were chocolates, I wanted them.

I peeled off each piece of tape, one at a time. This was my final present; I was going to make it last.

'C'mon, Sashi!' said Dad, 'Let's have a look! Get a wriggle on!'

I unpeeled the paper and passed it to where

Mum was hovering over me. She shoved it straight in her rubbish bag. The gift looked like a plain wooden box, but when I hinged it open, I squealed.

'Eeeee! Thank you!'

I planted a sloppy kiss on Dadu's cheek.

It was every colour you could think of – pens, crayons, pencils, chalks. Rubbers and paperclips, a little tray of paints with the world's tiniest brush.

'Well, if anyone deserves the full kit . . .'

Dadu and I always drew together. I even had my own special drawer at his house. Whenever we visited, he went straight to it to rummage for some shiny new cardboard, or a stack of thick tracing paper. Treasure. The drawer was stuffed with pens and felt tips and stickers, and all kinds of papers. He always kept each of the pens neatly in its box – none were ever missing and they never seemed to run out. Now I had a huge set all of my own, with everything I could ever need. I would *not* lose any of the lids.

'I need to try every single one of them! Right now!'

'Perfect for another masterpiece, eh?'

*'Dadu!'*

He always called my drawings that. He'd even framed some and put them up on his bookshelves and mantlepiece, squeezed up with the photos and beautiful wooden pictures and little boxes of . . . stuff. His photos were *ridiculous*. Mum and Dad had printed him plenty of normal pics, but it was always the school ones he had up: me looking scared stiff in an ugly brown cardboard frame.

I threw my arms around his soft belly and squeezed. 'Thanks, Dadu. I love it.' I really did.

'What a lovely gift,' said Mum, smiling at me and resting a hand on Dadu's shoulder. 'Sashi loves her stationery!'

'*Pooh!* Stationery!' Dadu edged forward on our sofa, 'It's all the worlds she's going to create!' He nudged the plain brown envelope towards me. His eyes all twinkly. 'Go on, go on.'

I took it and nestled deeper into his side.

Inside the envelope was a notebook. I leant over him to grab one of my new pens and Dadu sighed.

'Sashi, my Sashi . . . look here.' He swiped the book off my lap and opened it to show me. 'It's just a silly little thing,' he said, 'but your drawings always have stories, so I thought you could give comics a go . . .?'

He flipped through the pages one at a time. Most of them had rectangles all over, of all different sizes, but every few pages there was a little picture. *Oh!* Dadu had drawn it all himself. There was a character that looked just like me with stuff written above it, like: "And then she landed on the moon . . ." and "Sashi decided to eat one each of all her favourite foods . . ." and "The creature looked at her, and Sashi looked at the creature . . ."

I didn't know what to say, my brain was filling with pictures not words. I could do a burger, then sushi, then marshmallows. So many ideas! I just wanted to get stuck in. I gaped up at Dadu, tingling with joy, and he patted my knee. He knew.

'Right, let's take that bike for a spin, shall we?'

Surprise tears stung my eyes and I blinked quickly. I was so lucky to have a dadu like him. I was going to fill this book and be a comic book artist when I grew up, and I would have my own book in the shops, and I would have 'To Dadu' printed in the front like in real books, and I would give it to him; and we would have a big hug together.

For now, I hugged the sketchbook close, before placing it carefully on the coffee table and taking hold of my new handlebars.

'Sorry, Dadu,' I raised my eyebrows at him with my sternest look. 'You are NOT allowed on my new bike.'

# CHAPTER 6

## NOW . . .

I decided to call the octopus Ian.

It sounded good, right? *Ian the octopus*? Plus, he looked like an Ian; something about the slow, bobbity way he moved, the ripples in his big bulb of a head as he skulked from side to side in the back of the tank.

'You understand, don't you, Ian?' I whispered against the glass. '*You* would want me to help my Dadu.' I was still smarting from Darcie's refusal to plan Dadu's escape with me. Ian floated forwards. 'Are you any good at plans?' I asked him. 'I bet you are. What are you planning?'

We were back at the aquarium again. Apparently, they sold the season passes off cheap at the end of the year, so Mum and Dad had bought one for all of us last week. This was going to be our new Saturday afternoon "family time" ritual, to take our minds of where we *should* be, and what we *should* be doing. Like they could just swap Ian for Dadu and I wouldn't notice. At least Darcie would approve of the distraction.

'Ooh, just take a look at him. What do you think he's thinking?'

'Daaad!'

Dad had jumped up behind me and leant half his heavy body weight on me, squashing me completely. I'd laughed automatically, then cut it off when I remembered I was mad at him. We should be wondering what *Dadu* was thinking around about now, not this tentacly guy.

'Do you think he's psychic, like that octopus, Paul?'

'What are you even talking about?'

'Oh, you're too young to remember.' He was ignoring my snappiness. 'There was a famous octopus that predicted the results of all the World Cup games or something. Called Paul. Newspapers had a field day! Total rubbish, obviously. But you can see why people always draw aliens like them, can't you? The size of those brains. They certainly *look* telepathic.'

I tried to wriggle out from under him. '*My* aliens don't look like him.'

'True enough.'

In the comic strip I'd had published, my aliens were long tubes with eyes at each end. More like toilet rolls than octopuses.

'What's "telepathic" anyway?'

Dad started dancing around me, wiggling his fingers and talking in his spooky voice. 'He can read your miiiiind!'

*Wow. A mind-reading, future-predicting octopus? Cool.*

I rolled my eyes to hide how he'd impressed me, and Dad snapped back to normal. 'C'mon, you. We're not spending another day convening with octopi intelligence, we're going to have some fun. I've picked us up a treasure hunt!'

'Dad, I'm not seven.'

'Neither am I! But I wouldn't say no to a sunken hoard, huh? So let's go hunting!' He grinned at me and flapped a card decorated with pirates and mermaids right up in my face. I had to bat him away, but he looked all puppy-dog eager, so I softened. Also, I did quite like those treasure hunts. You sometimes got chocolate.

'We'll race your mum, we're bound to fill in the

card before her.' He started off into the Tropical Zone.

'No *way* she's doing it?! – Oh . . .' He turned and winked at me as he led the way. No, of course Mum wasn't doing it, banana-brain. The two of *us* doing it was ridiculous enough.

'Keep those eyes peeled young lady; gold coins, treasure chests, pearls – they're all for us – y'hear?' He was even putting on a pirate accent now. *Embarrassing.*

'Chill out, Dad.' I reached forward and took his hand, a giggle escaping.

We stormed round the aquarium on a mission, until Dad decided to stick his head in one of those glass dome things, designed for little kids to look inside the tank better. Something about the light, the water, whatever . . . it made him look just like Dadu.

The laughter died in my throat and I sank back against the nearest fake rock, guilty tears burning in my eyes. We were laughing and playing complete idiots in here, while Dadu was all alone, wondering where we were. Wishing for his family.

And he would love this. He was always the biggest child in the room. Like when he'd have me running around pretending to be a dog, then suddenly put on a fake stern face and say, "Enough fooling around now, Little Fish, you're not a child any more". Before barking out a belly laugh. I missed him so much it felt like hole in my tummy.

Dad unfolded himself awkwardly from the child-sized tunnel with a dumb grin. Then he frowned. 'One more, up you get. C'mon, we've nearly done the whole card. And I reckon it's back by that psychic octopus of yours . . . what did you say you've called him? Fred? Bob?'

'*Ian.*' I snapped. 'Dad, I'm not in the mood anymore.'

'One more, humour me.' His smile was gentle. 'Imagine how impressed your mum will be, eh? When I tell her I've convinced you to do this with me.'

I couldn't not smile at that. Mum's face would be a state – it would be worth it for that alone.

'I just feel guilty . . . having fun . . . when we should be . . . y'know.' I had a sudden picture in my mind of Dadu locked up in the old people's home like a jail – fingers pressed to the window.

The first time we'd visited him there, he'd looked so confused – all stranded in the wrong place. When he'd been in his little old house on Crew Lane, he used to constantly touch his things: those brown cardboard photo frames, my favourite wooden picture of a beautiful lady with ankle bracelets pulling a little wagon, the curved back of his carved wooden dinner chairs. His hands running over everything, as if he were remembering through his fingers. But seeing him propped in a wheelchair, in a blank room, was horrid. There were bits of his stuff scattered about, but it was nothing compared to the treasure cave of his own home. All white and beige instead of dark wood and jewel colours.

It was bad enough he couldn't really tell us how he was feeling any more, but he needed his photos . . . his *things*! He needed those little wooden peacocks from India that lived on the corner shelf and he always picked up and stroked when he was thinking. I hated the hospital brightness. And so many strangers! All swimming around in their own little worlds, while Dadu gazed out at them. I hated all of it. And now not even his family was there with him. And it was Saturday . . .

'What if he's expecting us?' I looked up at Dad.

'Oh, my love,' he pulled me into a tight hug just next to Ian's tank and sighed. 'He's not expecting us.' Then he pulled away and flicked the glass slightly.

'Pay more attention to this guy, huh? You don't catch him feeling guilty. Look at him, curled up in his wheel thing – happy as Larry!'

As Dad said that, the octopus sprung forwards – arms shooting towards Dad like weapons. Dad staggered backwards. 'OK, OK, maybe not. I was just making a point, don't mind me.' He fake saluted.

Then Ian did his sidewards scrolling move over to where I was stood. The way he moved sent waves of comfort through my body. I smiled at him. He clung to the glass looking right at me.

This time he was *definitely* trying to tell me something.

The thought was so strong it had to be real. *Oh man – the mind-reading thing!* As if to confirm it, the octopus bobbed, nodding.

Then a sensation passed over me like nothing I'd felt before. The back of my neck prickled, and I felt a cold sweat rising. I couldn't take my eyes off him – I was hypnotised.

This was *exactly* what Dad had told me about. From the newspapers.

But what was Ian trying to say?

***

It was real. It was really real.

As soon as I'd woken up, I'd reached for my sketchbook. And there it was, my drawing, exactly as it had come to me yesterday. Like a *vision*.

*Home.*

It was right on the page in front of me. There were Ian's babies. There was his ocean home, all wild and free. There he was, trapped in his tank like a jail. He looked so desperate to get out.

*Poor Ian.*

At the aquarium, I knew *something* had happened.

That weird feeling I'd had looking at him, like nothing I'd ever felt before. And all the way home in the car I'd been bugged by the sense that something important had changed, but I wasn't sure what it was. Just a little spark of excitement. I was carrying something special and secret – just me – and I had to look after it.

We'd found the last treasure hunt clue and claimed our prizes; both the chocolate *and* Mum's surprise. Dad tugged on my ponytail as I got in the car to give me an extra treasure-team wink, but I just wanted to get home and be by myself, with my secret.

As soon as I was alone, I'd started drawing.

It was so strange, I didn't even think what to draw, it just all came out. My hand moving, the pictures forming. Then I'd flopped into a heavy sleep. The rest of the evening was hazy – I must have put PJs on at some point – but now, everything seemed clear. And I had that magical drawing in front of me!

Ian had kids! I could see them; they'd come out of my pencil as if I'd looked at them with my own eyes. I'd drawn them in strange little pods, all lined up.

I stared at the picture of those pods in shock and shook my head. Why had I done that?

I grabbed my phone off my night table and sat cross-legged on my bed, sketchbook still propped on my lap. I searched-up "Octopus babies", but they didn't look right, then "Octopus eggs". Yes, eggs! The image results showed exactly what was in my comic – octopus eggs!

I ran my fingers over my drawing, frowning. Had I ever seen pictures like that before? NO. What was that word Dad had used for the mind-reading thing? Telephony? Teleporting? I'd known it the minute

I'd had that neck-prickling feeling, but now there was no doubt. Ian had sent me these pictures, and he needed my help.

He wanted to get back home to the sea. I *had* to help him.

I felt sick.

*Knowing* was OK and everything, but *doing* it? I couldn't. I mean, the total impossibility of it aside, I'd have to *steal* him. My heart beat faster at the word, and I blew a breath out slowly. *No way, too much.* But it wouldn't be like that, I was going to *free* him. Like in that old movie, *Free Willy*, when they set the orca loose in the ocean — with the punch and the jump and the splash — like that, but smaller. "Free" definitely sounded better. But still, not exactly easy.

And Mum and Dad could absolutely not know — they would 100% freak out.

So, *Challenge 1*: Keep it Secret.

I snapped the sketchbook shut and jumped out of bed. In the top of my wardrobe were a few old tote bags and I grabbed a couple of them and double-bagged the drawing before putting it back up on the top shelf.

*Challenge 2:* Build a Team

I'd half-watched enough of my dad's crime movies on Sunday afternoons to know that every great . . . er . . . *rescue* mission, needs a good team. With skills. What were my skills, beyond drawing? Communicating with octopuses! Hm. I wasn't about to share that with anyone anytime soon. I needed help.

Darcie, obviously. Getting her on board was going to be the tricky bit – this was NOT her kind of plan. Maybe some hard-to-resist charm would help? But could I really ask him? Did I even want him involved? I guess it would be nice to spend some time with him again.

I checked the time: 9 a.m. No one had plans on a Sunday; I was sure they'd come and meet me. I dressed warm then scooped my phone from where it'd toppled to the floor.

**NEW GROUP MESSAGE**

**ME:** Can we meet today? Beach at 12? Need your help with something.

**DARCIE:** Sashi, is this to do with your Dadu, because I thought we'd agreed?

**ME:** No! I promise it's not. Can you meet?

**DARCIE:** Of course, see you there.

**DARCIE:** Hang on, why am I in a group chat with Hassan?

**HASSAN:** Hey ladies, all set! See yous at 12 xx

**DARCIE:** ??

**ME:** Thank you! Both of you! See you there x

I knew I needed their help as clearly as I knew what Ian had been trying to tell me. Now, I just had to convince them to join me.

# CHAPTER 7

## TWO AND A HALF YEARS AGO . . .

'Hey Dadu, lift me up!'

I was too big. I'd been too big at eight, never mind ten. But these were our cherry trees, and this was what we always did. I couldn't see that blossom spreading above us and not want to do it. And extra special bonus: it would make Dadu laugh.

I jumped up and down on the spot, trying to grab a branch.

'I need a boost, Dadu!'

He looked across at me and smiled. 'Look at you!' he said. 'Such a big jump! Are you some kind of rocket ship?' Then he chuckled to himself and carried on walking.

I stopped still, staring at the back of his head as he walked away.

What was *that*? "Rocket ship"? *What?* He knew exactly what I was doing!

Had I missed something?

'Dadu, but you . . . Are you not going to do the thing?'

He turned and looked at me with a frown. I felt a bit sick.

'You know. You used to pretend you couldn't lift me, and now you really can't . . .?' With the fake grunting and straining. Like *always*.

I still had Dadu two days a week. He dropped me at school in the mornings and picked me up too. Years of cherry blossom walks stretching back in my memory – the petals falling like snow. Or snow falling like cherry petals. Or just rain sometimes, I guess. But Dadu-days always felt full of magic, whatever the weather.

This didn't feel magical.

And this was our favourite street at our favourite time of year; cherry trees on both sides, pink everywhere and smelling of sunshine. All the houses were painted a different pastel colour and the whole place looked like a cartoon street, in a perfect cartoon world. I drew it all the time.

Suddenly, Dadu beamed.

'For your mother!' He swung his finger in the air like this was some kind of revelation.

I *guess* for Mum. We always snapped off a tiny sprig, took it home and popped it in a glass on the dining table for when she got back.

I ran a couple of steps to catch him up, but my school bag bumped heavily into my hip, so I walked again, but faster. *It's fine*, I told myself. I was trying not to be cross, even though he had just ruined our game. *Just forget about it*.

I took his hand when I reached him. 'I would make a rubbish rocket ship, Dadu. I have no energy. What snacks do you have?'

He squeezed my fingers softly and patted them with his other hand as we stepped into the alley. The one where we usually ran a stick along the fence to make a good noise.

'Well, I'm sure I can find a little something, let me see.' He stopped and swung his little rucksack round to the front and pulled out a bag of iced gems. He was smiling, but he looked kinda sad. I definitely wouldn't ask for a stick.

He put a warm arm round my shoulder and squeezed. 'My good girl.'

I sucked on a pink gem and let it all turn to a sugary

mush in my mouth as we walked home in silence, and then swallowed it. The next one I crunched through. I saved all the blue ones till last and ate them in a rush just before we got to the house.

'Don't tell your mother,' Dadu grinned at me.

She would *not* approve of iced gems.

\*\*\*

On my next Dadu-day, a week later, I decided I didn't want to go past the cherry trees. I didn't want to talk about it, I just wanted to go a different way. Anyway, Dadu and me loved going on "longcuts". They were our very own invention.

As soon as my teacher gave the nod, I dashed from the front of the queue and hung on to Dadu's side, threading my arm through his and catching him up on my day.

'Someone's happy!' He smiled.

'Let's "longcut", Dadu! The fancy toyshop! With the mechanical plane and the wooden rainbow!'

I sounded more enthusiastic than I felt, but I wanted to get Dadu excited. I usually just watched and waited at the toyshop, as Dadu tried to interest me in everything. But I hated falling in love with stuff we weren't going to buy.

'Oh, I'm not su—'

'You *love* that one!'

'I don't think so, my Little Fish.' He frowned and we started walking.

Well, the beach was always a winner. It was nowhere near on our way, but Dadu liked it the best. "Stepping into the sky!" That was what he always said as we left the crowded, messy streets and everything opened up.

I threw my arms round his neck. 'Let's go and see the old railway line . . .?' I giggled. 'You can never see it too many times! I need to see the lines under the pebbles!'

I should be an expert on stilts and wheels and rails by now – the amount of times we'd visited – but instead Dadu's words had always swirled around me and I found myself just listening to the sound of his voice, gentle as spring waves, washing over me.

'Best we go straight back,' he said now. More of a gust of wind than a spring wave.

I didn't say anything.

Every road we passed, I peered down hopefully – eyes open for a tempting-looking shop front. Then I spotted the Indian supermarket – perfect!

I tugged on Dadu's arm. 'Dadu, isn't it nearly mango

season? Shall we go and see if they've got any in yet?'

He would *never* be able to resist. It was probably a bit early for mangoes, but we could always have a rummage in the spices.

His arm tensed in mine, and he looked down and shook his head as if the side road was scary.

*Dadu! C'mon! Really?*

'What did you have for lunch today, Little Fish?'

I looked up to see if he was joking, but his face still looked flat and weird. We'd walked past the supermarket now.

'Er . . . pizza, Dadu. I told you already, remember? And Cathy picked off all her pepperoni and I ate it?'

'I must remember to get something out the freezer for tomorrow,' he said.

'Are you going to have pizza, too?'

'Eh?'

'Never mind, Dadu.'

It was as if he wasn't listening to me at all.

He always listened. He always adventured. He always loved a trip to the Indian shop. I was worried. This felt like a big deal. Something important, like he needed my help.

I had to talk to Mum about it.

I got my chance that night as we were packing up the dishwasher. Dadu had gone home as soon as Mum was back from work, not stopping for food.

'Mum, Dadu's been acting all weird.'

'Weird how, Sashi-love?'

'I don't know. He's all *serious*. And . . . scared, almost. And it was like he didn't even remember our game at the cherry tree last week!'

She stroked my head. 'He's not a young man, Sashi – you need to go easy on him. We can't all have your razor-sharp mind!'

She ruffled my hair and grinned.

*Razor-sharp mind?*

I carried on scraping dinner off the plates and loading them up.

'Does that mean I'm clever?'

Mum laughed. 'Yes, my darling. You're the brightest little button I know.' She started tickling me so unexpectedly I nearly dropped a plate.

The next week, Dadu forgot to pick me up from school completely.

## NOW . . .

At a quarter to twelve I was on our beautiful beach, ready to meet Darcie and Hassan. I was where poor Ian should be, looking out over endless grey-blue sea, while he was probably on his fake bit of sand, or hiding in his wheel, yearning for his lost family. He needed my help, just like Dadu had. That time, after our walk home, I'd known something wasn't right with Dadu and I hadn't done anything. Now it was Ian's turn for help and this time I wouldn't be distracted. I would not let him down.

But what would Darcie and Hassan think?

I stomped the tideline, picking up all the cuttlefish bones until I had way too many to carry. How would I convince them? It was too much to ask. I sank to squat on my heels and laid the bones in a circle, making a chalk-white sunshine on the pebbles.

Some of the bones had browned round their thin edges, or snapped into pieces, but a couple were still perfect white ovals glinting in the September light. They looked so out of place; so un-sea-creature-like. Strewn across the beach, their crisp, shiny, whiteness stood out from all the browns and yellows and pinks around them like litter; something we should pick up on school trips to the beach with bin bags and gloves on.

There seemed like a never-ending supply of cuttlefish washing up their bones on our beach. You'd think the sea would be thick with them, swilling round your ankles as you paddled. Why had I never wondered this before? I'd never even considered what they looked like, until I'd seen one – seriously weird, that was the answer. There was one in a tank right next to Ian. They were both "cephalopods", apparently.

**FACT: Octopuses have eight arms, and cuttlefish have eight arms and two tentacles – tentacles only have suckers on the ends.**

I was learning a lot.

I got up and walked to the foamy edge of the water.

The sea was so calm today it looked like silk. You could see the bottom easily. Were they lurking there? With their creepy, beardy, tentacled faces? Were there octopuses in there too, exploring the seabed? I leant out over the gently lapping waves, peering down.

'Rarrrh!'

I leapt forwards landing with a splash. *'Darcie!'* I tried to scuttle away from the water but I was too slow and the next wave ran over the toe of my Converse. The icy water soaked through the fabric. 'Oh-oh-oh! So cold! Oh, you're evil!'

I turned with a laugh and grabbed the front of her coat, yanking forwards. 'There's no way you're coming out of this dry!'

If *I* was going to have ice-toes, Darcie could sure as hell have ice-toes too.

'I'm sorry!' she shrieked. 'I surrender! Also . . .' She looped her arms round me and lifted me clean off the beach, swinging me round, away from the sea. 'You're gonna get wet like a washed dog! And I'm wearing boots. So . . .' She plonked me down and shrugged apologetically at her feet.

*Good point.*

She had her chunky Doc Martens on. In fact, she was looking a bit pop star. Fluffy leopard-print jacket, skinny jeans. Not her usual Sunday beachwear.

'Sorry for your wet foot,' she guffawed, clearly not sorry. 'So, what are we here for Sash-attack? Have you spoken to your parents? Are you still considering that plan?'

*Plan?*

*Oh, to check Dadu out of the care home.*

'I told you I would leave it, so I'm leaving it, OK?' A bubble of irritation swelled in my chest.

Darcie reached out and grabbed my hand, interlocking fingers as we started walking back up the beach. 'But you'd tell me, right? If you changed your mind? Just because I don't think it's the best idea, doesn't mean I wouldn't help you. I would rather know and, you know, help and stuff . . .'

'Darcie, I—'

'That's the point of being best friends, isn't it? We don't have to agree on everything, but I'm always here for you.'

'Oh. Well, that's good.' The glow was almost enough to warm my ice-cold toes. I nudged her sideways.

'And I invited Hassan today for *you*, by the way . . . so you can claim your place as queen of the cool gang!' She pulled away from me in pretend horror.

I wanted her to deny it, but who was I kidding? She was super interested in him at the juice bar, and now dressed all fancy.

'What are you even on about?' she laughed. 'He's YOUR dreamily uncombed toddler playdate!'

Then she kicked a stone. 'You know I'm not interested in all that "in-crowd" rubbish.'

She looked hurt. I needed to bring back the silly. I flicked her shoulder. 'Tell that to your super-fluffy jacket!'

'*Why* are we talking to jackets?'

Me and Darcie both span around at the voice, then turned to face each other open-mouthed. HASSAN. *How much had he heard, exactly?*

'Oh, hi.' I tried to sound bored and irritated. It was what Hassan would expect from me. 'Darcie just likes talking to her fur coat because deep down she thinks it's still alive.' I didn't really manage to keep a straight face.

'It's fake! Sashi, you know it's fake.' Darcie widened her eyes at me then turned to Hassan. 'It's not real fur,' she said, cheeks pink, adding ridiculously, 'I don't talk to my clothes.'

I was giggling enough by this point I had to sit down.

'Okaaay then,' said Hassan, smoothing a fancy looking raincoat on the pebbles, then perching cross-legged on top of it. 'So, you two are weird.'

This was exactly why Hassan was Hassan and me and Darcie were, well, me and Darcie.

'Why are we here?' he continued.

'Yes!' blustered Darcie, sending me a silent plea for help as she tried to regain her cool. 'What's the big secret that needs face-to-face?'

Both of them were staring at me now. Darcie was so focused on me, and pointedly NOT on Hassan, she was burning holes in my skin.

Time for an explanation.

How had I not planned a way to bring this up? I couldn't possibly just come out with it . . .

'Just spit it out, Sashi. Whatever it is, I'm sure we can do something to help.'

Hassan looked uncertainly at Darcie, then nodded. 'Er, yeah – yeah, sure. We'll help.'

A tiny frown passed across Darcie's face, but then she smiled. 'Er . . .?

'OK!' *Stay focused. There's no getting out of this now.* 'This is going to sound strange. I think. I want you to know you don't have to be part of this if you don't want to, but I'm doing it either way – whether you're on board or not.'

I paused, but no one said anything, they just seemed to lean into the moment, waiting. I picked up a stone from the beach and passed it from hand to hand, I couldn't look at them.

'It's the octopus. From the aquarium. I want to set him, well, y'know . . .' I glanced up to see their expressions had changed to total confusion.

'. . . I want to set him free.'

*** 

Darcie's and Hassan's faces were both saying the same thing.

One word.

Wordlessly.

*"WHAAAT?"*

Understandable . . . perhaps I should back up a bit, tell them more about Ian.

'Hang on, hang on, hang on.' Darcie's eyes were closed and she was shaking her head, classic brain reset. 'Our aquarium here? The one down the road?'

'Er, yeah.'

'The octopus?'

'Yeah.'

'Free?'

'Er . . . yep.'

'As in, into the sea? This sea?'

'Well, I'm not going to set him free in the forest, Darcie. Of course the sea!'

'Yeah, I'll do it,' said Hassan with a shrug.

Darcie opened and shut her mouth a few times. She wasn't used to someone else making the call. Neither was I. I stared at him. Was he joking? He mainly looked bored, rubbing his hands on his knees. I gave him a gentle shove. 'Are you teasing me?'

'What? No! Why?'

'Well, why "yes"?'

'That's what you brought us here for, right? To ask us to do this? So yeah, sure. If you wanna do it, let's do it. No big deal. I said I'd help you whatever, so there you go.'

'Oh, thanks.'

'Besides, I could do with something else going on at the moment. I'm a bit sick of hanging out with the lads all the time, if I'm honest. A change would be nice.'

'It's a bit more than a change though, isn't it?' Darcie's voice was tight as a wire. She pulled her knees to her chest and buried her face in them, tugging her jacket around, before emerging looking pained. 'I mean, it's steali— Oh! And how would we even . . . Argh!'

She reached out and grabbed my hands, staring straight into my face with wide eyes. 'Do you really want to do this, Sashi? Do I even want to know why?'

'I'm not sure I can explain.' Should I tell her about the drawings and messages from Ian? No. She wouldn't understand. My heart squeezed shut as I decided not to say. 'I know I need to do it, though.'

'Well, I guess we're doing it then.' She smiled a lopsided smile, holding one of my hands out in front. 'Do we shake on it.'

'Oh c'mon, you two, hands in.' Hassan thrust his on top of ours making a three-way pile in the middle of our huddle. 'We need a team name or something. Or we could just say "Free the octopus",'

'His name's Ian,'

Darcie swung round smiling. 'Seriously?'

'Don't mock! Ian the Octopus. I think it's very dignified.'

'*OK* then.' Hassan's eyes were twinkling with amusement. 'On three. "Free Ian" – you ready?'

'I am *so* not doing this,' Darcie's pale long fingers were now limp between mine and Hassan's big hand as she rolled her eyes.

'Darcie,' her name sounded weird in his voice, 'you're doing this. On three. One, two . . .'

'FREE IAN!' we all finished.

'Ha! You *said* it,' I laughed – both at her joining in and her reluctant voice as Hassan threw her hand high.

'Now what?' laughed Darcie.

I was a bit stumped.

'To be honest, today's plan was to start chipping away at you both.' I shrugged. 'I thought it would take a bit longer.'

'We're here for you, Sash, no probs.' Hassan stood up. 'Let's go get it, shall we?'

Darcie looked up at Hassan – staring wistfully out to sea – and back to me, mouthing, '*what the . . .?*' silently.

'The point being . . .' she said, in an extra-loud voice. 'You don't need to do any persuading. It's fine. It sounds like a . . . good project. Something we can get really stuck into. Very distracting . . . for . . . er . . .'

*Distracting? Here we go again. Don't think about Dadu. Find a distraction . . .*

'. . . Hassan.'

*Oh.*

'Who sounds like he wants some entertaining. Amirite?' she shouted up at him. 'Oh, considering-the-horizon-one? I thought you wanted "something else going on", so there's no point stomping over there right now, is there? Besides, do you think we can walk in with a fishing net and then swagger right back out?'

'Ha! Hey . . .' He looked down at us, his face lit up with glee. 'What about a baby buggy?'

'A what-now?'

'Y'know, that clip. The video. CCTV or something. Did you guys not see that? Was that an octopus? Shark!! It was a shark. These bros stole a shark from an aquarium by putting it in a baby's pushchair or something. Don't you two watch the news?'

'YouTube isn't the news, Hassan.'

*Ouch.* 'Look, I don't want to *steal* anything, OK? Ian needs to be *rescued.* This is different.'

'OK, Sash-a-lac, but look . . . you have to admit there are some, er, similarities. Or that some people will see it that way, at least. And, y'know, technically—'

'Look,' I cut in. *La la la!* 'Thanks for saying you'll do it and everything, but I actually don't want you to decide right now. How about we take a week or something, come up with some pros and cons, make sure you're happy – OK? Then meet again.'

I suddenly wanted to stop talking about it.

We all walked to the road and Hassan forced us to land some "Team Ian" fist bumps. Then we went our separate ways.

***

I got the first note during Monday's P.S.H.E.

Ms Woking was soft, and encouraged "all forms of communication", so even Darcie felt safe to risk it. I stared at the folded note, written in dark red caps and titled, "**CON**". Darcie's handwriting. Even her capitals were so obviously her. I opened it carefully, shielded by my doodle-covered workbook.

**CON: It's going to be virtually impossible.**

*Great.* I scrunched up the slip of paper and shoved it in my trouser pocket, then shot a look over my shoulder to where Darcie sat at a table at the back. Ms Woking never let us choose our own learning partners. We had to "mix".

Darcie shrugged at me, like, "Well, it is!" Then she tapped Elsa on the shoulder and thrust another message at her. Elsa rolled her eyes and glared at me, as if I was the one asking her, and then passed it with the very tips of illegally polished purple nails to Niamh. I grabbed it and span back to the front.

**CON: We could be arrested.**

Followed straight away by:

**CON: Our parents will be seriously unimpressed.**

I felt sick. The notes got scrunched and I kept my eyes forward.

The next day the paper-attack continued. Tuesday was assembly and I could feel the Mexican-wave of movement flow along the line before I saw the red ink.

**CON: We know very little about octopus transportation.**

**CON: How will we get into the aquarium?**

For the rest of the day, they kept coming. All in red. What had I expected? The whole plan was seriously outside Darcie's comfort zone.

**CON: How will we get into Ian's tank?**

**CON: How would we get back out of the aquarium?**

Wednesday morning was P.E. Athletics. Matteo jogged towards me, shoved a scrap into my hand and jogged off. Like relay practice. I glanced down — it was black, not red! I smoothed it out hopefully.

**CON: Can you pair cut it out with all these flipping NOTES? It's embarrassing.**

*What??*

I twirled on the spot to see where it had come from and Hassan's eyes found mine, wide and pleading as he plunged into a hamstring stretch.

*I guess Darcie hasn't just been paper-bombing me, then.*

One of those boys – was it Luka? – shoulder nudged him with a laugh and pointed in our direction. More boys laughed. Hassan stared into the trees. I could see the pink on his cheeks from here. So, not the moment for a 'Team Ian' fist bump!

I slapped the paper into Darcie's hand as she jogged on the spot next to me.

'This is for you, CON-queen.'

She took it off me and then laughed happily. 'Ooh, that reminds me . . .' she plucked another crisp note from the waistband of her runners.

**CON: We would probably have to feed it something. (Eep!)**

I groaned, 'Darcie, can't we just tal—'

'Mmmmm!' Lips pressed together, her eyes widened in mild panic as Mr Fenlock approached. Her jog stepped up to sprint speed.

I was more than a little amazed to get another one in Hassan's writing the next day, via a sneery looking Francesca:

**CON: Do octopuses even live in English seas? Isn't it too cold?**

I nudged Darcie, gobsmacked.

'I know, right?' she whispered. 'I told him if he didn't join in, I'd start drawing hearts on them!'

I giggled. Poor Hassan, he was like a hostage. Although when had they been chatting without me?

At home time, there was one in my bag. No hearts.

**CON: We're supposed to be focused on finding work experience placements this term.**

That was definitely Darcie, and she was getting off-topic. I felt numb. I didn't have answers to any of this. They were obviously going to change their minds. Should *I*?

Back home, I took my sketchbook down and

looked at the picture; Ian yearning for his egg-babies, trapped in his tank and dreaming of freedom. How many people had he tried to communicate with before he finally got through to *me*? I was his only hope. I had to do this, even if it was by myself. The loneliness gripped like ice.

During Friday registration another note came round. I nearly didn't open it, then I noticed the blue ink seeping through the paper.

**FACT: Octopuses have BEAKS, like BIRDS. They use them to crack shells!!**

Oh, good sign! Research meant she'd started to get interested. Also — beaks? — what the hell?

Then came another note, a green one.

**PRO: We love Sashi ♥♥♥♥**

**PRO: (Easy there D.) It will definitely be interesting.**

*D??*

**PRO: We can treat it as a science project.**

Then a separate note they'd obviously both written together at some point.

**WE NEED TO MEET IAN.**

# CHAPTER 9

'Don't. Tap. The glass.' I tried not to grab Hassan's arm – he was making me nervous.

'Hey, chill out, OK? But does he come out at all, or is he just that ball of jelly back there?' He pressed his nose right up against Ian's tank, his breath misting the glass as a gaggle of small children waited behind him.

Ian didn't move.

'Soooooo . . .' Darcie took ten steps back, and I already knew everything she was going to say. Coming back and seeing the plan through her eyes was painful. 'Is this tank, like, completely sealed into the wall then?'

'Yeah, I know, it does look a bit like that, doesn't it?'

'Don't be daft, you two, they've got to clean it and stuff somehow, haven't they?' Hassan was still pressed to the glass; Ian was still skulking in his wheel. I didn't think the two of them were going to be friends.

I closed my eyes tight.

*Come on, Ian. Speak to Hassan and Darcie. You can trust them.*

I opened one eye hopefully.

Nothing.

Why would he just speak to me and not anyone else? I guess he'd seen how sad I'd been, maybe he thought we could help each other. I felt a warm spark in my chest. *Thanks, Ian.*

But, warm spark aside, right now he was barely visible. Not good. Even the little kids had given up and moved on.

'What's *this* crazy creature?' Hassan had moved on too.

'A cuttlefish.' I tried to keep the disappointment out of my voice.

'No way! Like the white shell things on the beach? How do *they* match *this*?'

'I don't really kn—'

'They only have one bone.' Darcie put an arm round each of our shoulders. 'So, we should probably scope the fire exits. Check the security. I'm stumped by this tank, I have to say. Maybe we should do a tour of the perimeter . . . what do you think?'

'I . . . yes. Those things. They all sound good.'

*Was she still on board, then?*

'Check the turtles! They have, like, *snake* necks!' Hassan pulled away from us and darted across to the opposite tank where some long-necked turtles were diving around. He looked as excited as a three-year-old.

Darcie folded her arms and followed him, her eyebrows raised. 'I guess those would be the "snake-necked turtles" then?' She tapped the info card.

'Alright smarty-pants!' I giggled. I felt a bit bad for how much she was teasing Hassan, but in all honesty, it seemed to wash right over him. Must be nice. 'Hassan, how have you not been here a hundred times already?' I asked.

He shrugged. 'Dunno. Just not one of those things we've done.'

'Well, you've got a season pass now,' said Darcie, waving the little credit card passes she'd picked up on the door – Hassan's photo face beamed out charismatically, Darcie's looked ominously like a police mug shot – 'you can come check out the fishies every day if you like.'

'Cool.' He nodded seriously, and I felt a warm glow for my old friend. I wasn't quite sure why I'd decided to rope him into this, but I was glad I had now.

Darcie paused too.

'Well, you should definitely take this then,' she passed him the card and shot me a look which I knew meant, *"I misjudged Hassan and now I feel bad. Fishes, eh?"* Her looks were very vocal like that. 'I'm going to pop to the gift shop,' she said. 'I feel the need for an aquarium-themed notepad for a "Team Ian To-Do List". You know stationary fixes everything . . .' She pulled a stupid face at me.

Gift shop! Oh yes!

Darcie's shelves at home were stacked with fancy stationary. Maybe that was the answer! Darcie was pretty much a winner at school, life and existence. I needed a fish-themed notebook too! Or maybe a fish rubber . . .

'I'll come with you, Darce.'

'Dudes, dudes, dudes. . .'

*'Dudes?'*

'Whatever. Look.' Hassan was studying the leaflet they'd given us on the door – I'd put mine straight in the bin. 'Octopus feeding: 2 p.m. Let's meet back for that.'

*Octopus feeding?* Someone else got to feed Ian? *Ugh.* Of course they did, but the thought of it still made me sick. *He's mine.*

I couldn't shake the bad mood as I rummaged through the gift shop's endless collection of tempting things. Suddenly it all seemed like rubbish and there was nothing I wanted. I sulked on the step and watched as Darcie examined every single notebook.

Let's be honest, neither of my friends were interested in Ian at all. And as soon as Darcie actually chose one of these books and wrote down that list of ridiculously impossible challenges, they were all going to look *too* ridiculous and *too* impossible. Everything was worse written down. "Alarm codes" and "perimeters", what were we even thinking? The whole plan was doomed.

My teeth squeaked and my tongue ran over a familiar texture. *Oops.* I was chewing on one of my ponytails, Mum would freak.

'Two oh five!' Darcie was patting me on the head. 'C'mon, c'mon.'

*The feeding.*

We rushed back to the tank and a small crowd had gathered. Hassan was right at the front next to a tall guy in an official aquarium shirt, who was droning on in a bored-sounding voice. It didn't look like any actual feeding was happening yet.

The guy in the shirt had really weird brown curly hair. It looked like he'd curled it himself. What was that about?

His glasses looked fake too – was he trying to look extra clever because he supposedly knew so much about octopuses?

Everything he was saying right now, he'd probably just googled.

He couldn't be a marine biologist or anything – he didn't look old enough. Eighteen, maybe? He was probably just on work experience.

What did he really know about Ian?

I hated him.

*'Sashi!'*

'Ow!'

Darcie had pinched my arm.

'What was that for?' I rubbed the tender bit, laughing nervously.

'You were in a total trance. I'd said your name about four times! We need to get closer, to see the feeding. Let's wiggle in.'

'Oh, sure.' We squirmed past some grown-ups with bulky pushchairs, trying not to squash any toddlers, and slipped in next to Hassan – close enough to see the total disinterest on feeder-guy's face. He was talking about octopus camouflage – clearly completely magical – as though he were doing a school report on a plate of salad.

**NEW FACT: Octopus skin doesn't just change colour, but also how reflective it is, how see-through it is AND its texture.**

Well, *I* was impressed with Ian's mad skills.

This guy wasn't even looking in the tank as he talked. The boring sound of his boring voice must scream "food" in octopus though, because from the corner of my eye I saw a movement from behind the glass, and a group of kids all "oohed" in chorus. Ian had floated right to the front again – all eight arms stretched wide, his skirt fully extended. Majestic.

Then his arms curled around something silvery floating in the water. A piece of fish! *Where had that appeared from?* He shoved it under the skirt-bit as another fish floated down from the top of the tank. *What? How?* So much for seeing how the food got in, it was appearing like magic.

Just as I was about to ask the bored guy, Ian's eyes rose to where I could see them and locked on to mine. A shiver ran from my scalp to my toes leaving a cold sweat behind it. I couldn't take my eyes from his. Something was happening.

Ian was talking to me again.

***

I'd sat for a while with the new message from Ian, cross-legged on my bed, sketchbook on my lap. It had come in a blur, just like the last one. I could barely believe it had happened again, that Ian had trusted me again. I was so grateful.

But *Ian*! This was serious. He was in danger. I'd *known* there was something up with that creepy guy, but this? This was next level. If freeing Ian had been the right thing to do before, now I knew it was necessary. We had no choice, and we had to be fast! Darcie and Hassan had to see that too.

That night, I messaged them the news.

**TEAM IAN GROUP CHAT**

**DARCIE:** I canNOT believe the keeper guy is actually poisoning Ian?!

**ME:** I know right? But I saw it with my own eyes.

OK, so I didn't *exactly* see it with my own eyes. But what else was I going to say? I put down my phone and picked up a pencil. That Ian had psychically communicated it to me? I couldn't! Darcie would NOT go for that. I knew what Ian had told me was real, but there was no way I could prove it right now. And Darcie liked proof.

My hand was moving fast as I waited for their response. Soon every scrap of paper on my bedroom desk was covered in skulls and crossbones, like a pirate invasion.

**HASSAN:** I totally buy it, did you see his hair?

**DARCIE:** ?? I think I'm missing the hair point?

**HASSAN:** It looked like he'd curled it himself.

I picked my phone back up.

**ME:** Yes!!! *And* his glasses looked fake.

**DARCIE:** Hello!? Relevance?

**HASSAN:** Completely relevant. Goes to character.

**DARCIE:** Er . . . who says that? And anyway, bad hair does-not-equal octopus-i-cide.

*"Octopus-i-cide"*?! Oh, like "homicide" – murder. She didn't believe he would try and kill him. *Hmm.* Maybe I would doubt it too if Ian hadn't made it clear as day to me. I needed to show Darcie and Hassan, the way Ian had shown me.

**ME:** Yeah, but poison does.

My fingers shook as I typed it, but I needed them with me on this. How was I going to do this? I stared blankly at my doodles and a shocking possibility flitted across my mind.

91

*I couldn't.*

*Could I?*

I knew what that hideous keeper-creep was doing, this would just help the others believe it too – make it easier for all of us. Don't overthink it. I ran downstairs and emptied out the under-sink cupboard. I'd been sure it would be full of things with hideous chemicals in, and warning labels on. It used to be, but Mum had obviously had a clean out. Every single bottle seemed to be some eco-product made entirely from plants and utterly lacking the thing I was looking for. Which was poison. What was I *doing*?

Maybe the bathroom. We cleaned our toilets with bleach, didn't we? Apparently not. My phone buzzed again in my pocket and my blood felt cold. I could feel doubt oozing from it in waves with each vibration. I unlocked it with a swipe of my thumb.

**HASSAN:** 10 points for octopus-i-cide D. I like.

All credit to Hassan, he really did seem prepared to take my word for anything. *The garage.* That was a Dad-zone. I slipped through the utility room, stepping into wellies as I went and shivering at the sudden chill.

The garage was a total mess – a storage cave of broken things. I often fantasised about the things we could do with it . . . carpentry workshop, art studio, sleepover den. It seemed such a waste to just use it as Dad's project graveyard.

But somewhere in here, there just had to be . . . BINGO! Rat poison. With a perfect skull and crossbones warning label.

*Buzz buzz.* Swipe.

**DARCIE:** We need to be certain though. We can't just accuse someone of this kind of thing without proof.

*It's coming Darcie*, I thought. *It's coming.*

The poison was at the back of a shelf, far enough away it would look glimpsed from a distance in a photo. What if he just denied it?

*Buzz buzz.* Swipe.

**HASSAN:** We don't need to accuse anyone of anything — we just need to FREE IAN.

Ha ha. Yes! Exactly, Hassan. No one else needed to know about this, just us. I took the photo, trying to make it blurry enough to look rushed but clear enough to make out the label, then checked to make sure there was nothing in the shot that screamed "garage" rather than "aquarium". Before I could change my mind, I sent the picture to the group chat.

**ME:** Guys, THIS is what I saw him put on Ian's fish.

Got pic as he was packing up.

Send.

I sank to the cold garage floor, head between my knees. My breath was coming fast, and it felt like I had three octopus hearts all beating inside me. *Ba-ba-ba-dum-dum-DUM.* But it was done.

*Buzz Buzz, Buzz Buzz, Buzz Buzz. Breathe, Sashi.*

**HASSAN:** Holy Moly.

**DARCIE:** Check you, Ace Ventura Pet Detective.

**HASSAN:** You what?

**DARCIE:** Never mind. 90s movie. You should be careful, Sashi. If this guy is up to something, we should all be careful.

Darcie was an expert on 90s movies. Quiz-team-special-subject level expert. When her aunt was babysitting, dinner was always a pizza in front of a cheesy old film. Which is why I always liked to visit when her mum was away. It's where I'd first seen Free Willy, the one about the kid who sets the orca free. That kid had to be careful too – the bad guys trying to hurt the whale nearly caught up with him. And he'd had to tell a few white lies.

**HASSAN:** Point.

**HASSAN:** But more importantly, we gotta get that jelly-sack outta there.

**ME:** Ha. Don't let *him* hear you call him that!

**DARCIE:** Er . . . we wouldn't want to offend octopus dignity!?

**ME:** Are we back on then?

**HASSAN:** Were we off?

I looked at my phone, skin prickling.

**ME:** No! You know what I mean! You're not put off by the scary guy!?

**DARCIE:** Free Ian all the way duuudes!!!!

**ME:** You idiot! I love you xxx

**HASSAN:** Have I mentioned that you two are strange?

**DARCIE:** Next Sat at the aquarium?

**HASSAN:** Can we make it Sunday, I've got training and like, two football matches Sat?

**ME:** Sure - and tomorrow night Darcie - don't forget

you're coming for dinner at mine! My Mum and Dad miss you. Vomit.

**DARCIE:** Don't be mean! I miss them too!

I put my phone back in my pocket and closed my eyes. What had I got into? The poison wasn't a lie, and we absolutely had to do something about it. But the photo. The fake photo. I couldn't really believe I'd lied to my friends like that. I just needed to make sure Darcie and Hassan *never* found out about this.

# PART TWO

# CHAPTER 10

Everyone was making an extra effort because Darcie was here. Mum was swishing around in a long skirt instead of wearing her usual saggy yoga trousers. Dad placed both hands flat on the table and looked at us as if he actually wanted to talk.

'Dad, where's your . . .?' I pretended to look on the floor, behind the bottle of chilli sauce. Faking panic. He started to look concerned. 'Dad, where's your phone?'

'Oh, stop it! We're having a family meal! It doesn't matter.'

'Ha!' He normally sat and shovelled in food with one hand, while scrolling with the other, barely even noticing Mum and me during dinner. Until he would read something, or remember something, that would set him off on a long anecdote about work, or someone we knew.

Tonight, he was all attention.

'And how are you, Darcie? How's your mum?'

Good gravy! The sooner this fakity-fake-fake meal was over the better, and me and Darce could get upstairs and do some much-needed plotting.

'Let the poor girl get some food first, Manu. Why don't you start serving up?'

Mum and Dad had cooked Bengali food, although the amazing smell just made me sad. They'd learnt these recipes from Dadu – Dadu always said nobody made luchi breads as soft as his and now there they were on the table and he wasn't here. I'd always thought he'd teach me too.

The table was filling up quickly – alur dom and delicious, sweet, cholar dal. A huge pot of rice. The smell was too much, seriously. There were even sondesh for after, Dadu's favourite. I'd seen the sweet little crumbly balls lined up in the kitchen earlier. Last year I would have been boxing some up to take round to him.

Dad filled our plates and for a few minutes we all ate steadily, lost in our own thoughts and the delicious food. At least it was a break from the Mum-and-Dad attack.

In fact, it was Darcie who spoke up first, finding my hand under the table and taking hold of it.

'How is Sashi's Dadu getting on? Is he any better?'

With her spare hand she dabbed her mouth with a paper towel.

My breath caught in my throat. She hadn't told me she was going to ask. She was always telling me to accept things as they were and trust Mum and Dad. Now this.

Mum paused eating and shot a look at Dad. Dad made a harrumphing, throat-clearing sound, then flashed Darcie a tight smile. 'It's sweet of you to ask, but I'm afraid he's not getting any better, no.'

It was his "subject-closed" voice.

Darcie's fingers squeezed mine; cool and dry. I felt dizzy. I'd tried to read my dad's face for clues as he spoke. We'd not actually spoken once about Dadu since that awful morning weeks ago. I'd thought about asking hundreds of times, but never knew quite how to bring it up. Once or twice, I was sure I'd heard Mum and Dad say his name when I was in another room, but whenever I got close they clammed up.

How did *they* know he was no better? Without seeing him! Was Dad just guessing?

Darcie's fingers tightened on mine. 'Did . . . did you

consider having him to stay here at all? Instead of the home?' Her voice shook – I'd never heard Darcie's voice shake before.

I flooded with gratitude, then guilt. I'd lied to her about the poison picture, I didn't deserve a friend like this. I whipped my plait into my mouth. Right now I needed to know what Mum and Dad were going to say. WHY wasn't Dadu here, where I could be with him and help him get better, and show him how much we loved him?

Mum smiled over at Darcie – her eyes glassy – then turned to me. I dropped the plait. It wasn't me who'd asked! I stared down at the tablecloth and started scratching at a crust of dried dal with my thumb nail. I could see Mum from the corner of my eye turn back to Darcie again. She sighed.

'Yes, we would have loved to have had him here, but it's so complicated.' Mum's voice was even shakier than Darcie's. 'It's not just us that he doesn't remember, it goes deeper than that. It's . . . more basic things.'

'I could help.' I spoke so quietly I'm amazed anyone heard me, but when I looked up, Mum,

Dad and Darcie were all staring at me. Mum and Dad looked horrified.

Darcie leapt in again. 'Are you worried he would wander off – go missing?'

'Have you read about that?' asked Mum.

'Yeah, a character in a book, I think.'

'Yes, it can happen. Sashi's Dadu never wandered, though. Maybe he would . . . maybe he would . . .' Mum drifted off. She wasn't answering the question. I looked up at her, and she caught my eye.

'He needs nursing, Sashi my darling. Round-the-clock nursing, that we just can't give. Going to the toilet, getting dressed. Swallowing his food so he doesn't choke.'

*He could choke?* I pushed my chair back with a spine-aching scrape. I didn't want to hear this.

'No, Sashi, listen. You've asked, and I think it's best you understand. People in the advanced stages of dementia, like your Dadu, sometimes forget to swallow, you know, things like that, it can be dangerous. They need their pain monitored. It's not as simple as forgetting what year it is, darling.'

*I could help – I could really help – but instead,*

*Mum was trying to scare me.* Tears stung my eyes, and my fingers gripped Darcie's tighter. I tugged her to her feet with me, shaking my head. *No.*

I wouldn't let Mum do this.

Mum smoothed her napkin on her lap. 'Darcie, it was lovely of you to ask after him, but as you can see it's very upsetting for all of us.'

'Sash, sit a sec,' Darcie pulled me back down. I couldn't see through the tears burning my eyes. I didn't need to. I could imagine the apologetic smile she was flashing my parents. The three of them radiated attention at me like three hot balls of light. I could feel my nostrils flaring.

'Has Sashi told you about our science project?' Darcie suddenly burst out. Her voice all loud and cheerful.

I wiped my eyes and nose on my sleeve as she started talking frantically, making out Project Free Ian was a school thing. Well, that would come in handy, there was no denying that.

Luckily, I had a pencil in my back pocket, so I scrawled away on my napkin while Darcie went off on one. Me and Darcie hanging in my room where

I wished I was. As the pictures formed in front of me, I felt the tension in my body give way a bit. When Darcie hit "cephalopod intelligence" I even managed a warning nudge – *doomed*. Dad had read that adult science book, she did *not* want to risk setting him off – but Darcie matched Dad fact for obscure fact, she'd clearly been doing her homework.

**FACT: Octopuses have blue not red blood, because the metal component of it is copper not iron, like ours.**

*Huh.*

*What was made of copper? Copper kettles!*

I drew an octopus with veins full of old-fashioned pots and pans.

You should have told us it was for school, Sashi!' Dad had been Darcie-d. She was irresistible to all parents . . . and she knew it.

'*Our daughter* only informed us that she no longer wanted to spend Saturday 'family time' with her family any more, Darcie, and she'd be going to the aquarium with friends instead.' Mum's raised eyebrows found me as a reminder of how THAT particular conversation had gone down. CLUE: not well.

'Which we said was totally fine,' my dad added quickly.

'Although it did rather undermine the whole concept of *family time*,' said Mum.

'But now we know it's a science project too! And she *is* twelve now.'

Were we really going to repeat the entire conversation again? Great. Dad had only just won the last time, and I think he was half-heartedly on my side at best. I needed a distraction.

'We're doing the project with Hassan.'

'Oh, so *that's* why you're hanging out with Hassan again. That makes a bit more sense.' I'd talked to Mum a bit about him after school last week.

'I hear *you* and he are getting on rather nicely, Darcie?' chipped in Dad, in full on teasing-uncle voice.

'Er, what?'

'Dad!'

The look Darcie gave me almost wasn't funny. It kinda looked like she was mad.

I beamed her my best look of apology. 'I just told *Mum* that you were both getting on better than I thought you would.'

'That *was* a private conversation, Manu.' Mum gave Dad a look that could silence a hurricane and yet somehow he still carried on talking, chuckling like a robot Santa.

'And he calls you "D", I understand? That's where it starts, y'know. Before you realise it'll be—'

'Dad!'

'Manu!'

It was Darcie's turn to push back her chair and stand up. 'Thank you so much for a delicious dinner, Mrs Dutta.'

'Helen, please. And please ignore Sashi's dad – he likes pretending to be a teenager every now and again.'

'Hahaha,' *fake laugh*. 'No, not at all. It was wonderful. But me and Sashi had better get on with our project.' *Fireball eyes*.

I felt terrible. Darcie had just asked what I'd been desperate to ask myself, and I'd repaid her by embarrassing her. An image of the fake poison picture flashed through my mind, betrayal on top of betrayal. I picked up the doodle I'd been drawing, ripped it in half and shoved it in my pocket – I was a horrible friend.

# CHAPTER 11

## ONE YEAR AGO . . .

I was plonked in the middle of my new school's steps as everyone flowed past. Big groups of friends parting round me as if I were a rock in a river. I didn't care. No one had any idea who I was anyway.

School was such a waste of time right now – I needed to be with my Dadu. I couldn't believe I'd made such a fuss! The guilt was so heavy I felt like I'd never stand up again. I'd just have to sit on these filthy school steps all year.

That look on his face!

I swiped my wrist across my eyes to mop up some of the tears and tried to breathe through it, like I knew Mum would tell me to do.

*Eyes closed, big breath in.*

I could hear the mummer of a thousand conversations around me. All the friends I hadn't made yet.

*Breathe out.*

Mum always joked that Dadu was my best friend. I'd only ever had one BFF, back in Infants, but she'd suddenly ditched me for no reason and then turned some other girls against me. It was safer to keep to yourself. Hassan didn't count – his primary school was across town from mine. And it wasn't like I didn't have *any* friends anyway – I chatted to everyone.

I wasn't really lonely. But it was true I couldn't talk to anyone in the way I could talk to Dadu. So what if he was my best friend? He always had something funny or interesting to tell me, and he would never ditch me.

The thought made a fresh stream of tears escape my closed eyes. Who was I kidding? I couldn't really talk to Dadu any more . . . not like I used to. We didn't have our days together now of course – no one gets picked up from secondary school by their grandparents, do they? Besides, I had to catch a bus. And, let's face it, Dadu was getting worse. A lot worse.

I gave up on the deep breathing with a huff and opened my eyes.

*Oh heck!*

It was that Darcie girl – of all the people! I glanced around for somewhere to hide, but I was miles from any useful embarrassment shelter. She was heading straight for me.

Week one I'd decided she was by far the dopest girl in my year. Secondary school had been a shocker. It was clear I couldn't chat with *everyone* any more, there were just too many people. *And* some of them seemed proper mean. A gang of boys had been teasing this Darcie for sitting at the front, always having her hand up. One had shouted at her that she needed glasses to look the perfect "swot" part. She'd turned round with a flick of her long blonde hair and said proudly, "I *do* look the part! I *am* the part, silly". She'd owned it. Completely.

So I'd been avoiding her ever since.

Now crying on a step!

Any sensible person would run the other way from me, but she slowed down as she approached. *Bag. Rummage. Look busy.* I grabbed my rucksack and dragged it towards me.

'Hey,' she said, plonking herself down. She gathered all her hair together behind her neck then placed it over her shoulder, removing the one natural barrier between our faces. There was nowhere to hide.

'Hey.' I smiled. Sniffed. Snuck a quick glance up at her.

'Have the idiots been giving you trouble?'

'What? Oh! No . . . I'm fine.'

She raised her eyebrows. 'Well. Good. Cos this whole school thing is trickier than I'd imagined it would be.'

'Really? You seem to be doing OK.'

She laughed. 'Good.'

A second passed. What was I supposed to say?

'It's not school anyway. Don't worry, it's all fine.'

She turned to me, her eyes circling my face.

*Yes, I get it. I don't look fine.*

'Look, honestly. No one is bothering me. Thanks for stopping and everything,' I blurted, then added, 'it's really kind.'

'So . . .?'

She let it hang there. Did she really want to hear my sob story? She didn't seem about to go anywhere.

Somehow, I started telling her all about Dadu. That the doctor had said it was probably dementia. How it had started a year or so ago but now seemed to be getting loads worse, really suddenly. How he'd started to get all grumpy and sad with me. Little things. Or he'd just sit still with a look on his face like someone had died and you had to get his attention to snap him out of it, but then he'd pretend nothing was wrong. How he would bump into things. Right up to what had happened last night.

She had her hand on my knee now and didn't seem to mind we were right in the middle of the steps, blocking everyone's path.

'So, what happened? You were playing Lego . . .?'

'Ugh, it's such a tiny thing, you're going to think I'm an idiot.'

'I don't think you're an idiot.'

'We've been working on a space station together . . .'

I shot her a defiant look, but she swung her knees into mine.

'. . . and?'

'Well, he couldn't make the pieces fit – Dadu can *always* make the pieces fit.'

She shifted slightly on the hard concrete. I wasn't explaining right.

'He's an engineer!' I shrugged. 'It wasn't just that

though. He got really angry . . . he was just, like, trying to get this light brick into the research lab module, and he was pushing it harder and harder and then . . . he, like . . . *grunted* and threw it across the room.'

My chest was squeezing tighter. His *face*. It had been all scrunched up and angry looking. He didn't look like him. *My* Dadu was nearly always on the edge of laughing – a twinkle in his eye as he teased me about something. But not *this* guy. I'd just stumbled to my feet in the living room, sobs blocking up my throat. Making a big fuss. But I needed to get out of there! I'd shut myself in my bedroom.

I didn't want to tell this Darcie that bit. She seemed like someone who would never dream of running off to her room.

'He shouldn't have thrown it like that! If it'd been me, I'd have been in so much trouble!'

It wasn't *my* fault the stupid thing was so fiddly.

Darcie put her arm around me. 'It sounds really upsetting. You must have been shocked.'

'Yes! Well, kind of. I was . . . but . . . it's just, I feel so *guilty*. I *was* shocked, but I made such a fuss! And then he came up to my room later, offering the stupid light brick like an apology.' My voice had gone all wobbly.

I took a shaky breath, remembering.

'Look,' he'd said, 'look it's here Little Fish, I found it. I'm so sorry. I just, I just . . . I don't know. But *look* – here.'

The brick sitting on his outstretched hands, his eyes pleading.

'Please forgive me, Sashi. Although, unforgivable . . . I know, I know. But it's not lost. You can put it in yourself. We're so nearly finished now, aren't we? It's going to be magnificent . . .'

I turned my face away from Darcie.

'He thought I'd been sad about losing the stupid brick!' I told her.

Had I been? Was that it?

'Hey, I know I don't know you, but I think I get it. I'm really sorry.'

I shook my head. 'You *don't* get it.' *Why was I telling this girl all this stuff?* 'I didn't tell him it was OK! I took the brick and shut my door on him. Then he went home before we even had dinner. We never argue.'

'So now you know, right?' She swivelled on the step to face me full on. 'From what you've told me, it sounds like he's going to start behaving differently a lot. And you love him.' I wasn't even trying not to cry now. 'But we're only eleven!' She laughed then stopped suddenly, looking sheepish. 'We're going to mess up sometimes. And he loves you too. So it's OK. Just be dead nice to him next time you see him.'

How did she make it sound so simple? But I could do that. I would spoil him. It would be OK.

'Ugh!' I wiped my face and stood up. 'Thanks. You're right. Let me know if you ever need a pep talk about anything!' I tried to laugh, but it came out more like a cough.

'How about you sit by me in maths instead? I could use an ally.'

*A what?* Who cared. I grinned, but shrugged. *Play it cool.* 'Yeah, all right.'

Maybe it was time I had a proper best friend after all.

# CHAPTER 12

## NOW . . .

***

Darcie, me and Hassan were sitting in silence under the school's single tree – a big oak on the scrubby bit of grass behind the lower years' playground – and Darcie still wasn't talking to me. It had been nearly a week since the dinner disaster at my house.

We were the only kids to be seen. Firstly, because nobody else was daft enough to be outside when it was this cold, and secondly, because this was the most back-end corner of the school possible. No surprise it was Hassan's suggestion.

'Looking on the bright side,' he said, 'I have more clue what the hell's going on without the girl chat, so that's something. And it's more peaceful.' He started whistling as he rolled a fallen acorn between his palms, cracking its shell.

We still had a rescue mission to plan, but the silence thing made the planning thing a bit tricky. I started scrubbing through the fallen leaves around us, looking for my own acorn fiddle toy.

I'd only told Mum the truth – the two of them *were* getting on a bit well, seeing as it was Darcie's mantra to "never trust the cool kids".

It wasn't my fault Dad had twisted it up completely.

'So, which one of you chatterboxes has the notebook thing? With the list?'

Neither of us said anything. I looked down at my filthy hands – no acorn and now black nails, great. I could hear the sound Darcie made when she sucked in her cheeks and sneaked a glance. Hassan swung from side to side, gawping first at me, then Darcie.

'You did *do* it the other night, right? After your little family dinner date? The master plan of action?'

'No.' Darcie paused.

*Was that it?*

'We didn't get round to it. Sashi had other things on her mind that she felt the need to talk to everyone about.'

'Oh c'mon! I wasn't talking to everyone about *anything*. I wish you'd just forget about it. It was honestly *nothing*.'

'I think *I* can decide if my own feelings count as *nothing* or not, thank you, Sashi. But thanks for diminishing them anyway.'

'Dimini – what-now?'

*'Kay then.'* Hassan held up a palm to each of us,

acting the referee. 'So, I take back that bit about knowing what the hell's going on!'

He laughed and I glared at him.

I was running out of ideas with Darcie.

Upstairs on Monday night, I'd gone for the obvious Option 1) apologise, but she'd been pale with rage; it was scary. She'd just connected straight to my speaker and put on some music.

'I'm going to leave this playing long enough for your parents to think we're doing something up here,' she'd said. 'But I can't talk to you right now.'

She'd taken a book out of her bag and sat on my bed. I'd tried to thank her for asking about Dadu, but when she shot me a look there were tears in her eyes. She looked away again so quickly any chance to talk about it was shut straight down. I really was so grateful for what she'd done at dinner, it ached that she wouldn't let me thank her for it.

She'd read for half an hour in silence, then packed up and left.

At school she'd avoided me. It had been coming, let's face it. I knew the more she hung out with the likes of Hassan, the less she'd be interested in me.

I'd tried Option 2) strings and strings of text apologies. Nothing. Except some rubbish about "needing time". Option 3) I'd cycled to her house and pushed a comic of us through the letter box. I think maybe that one had worked a bit, because that was yesterday. And then this morning before school, Hassan had messaged to suggest this meet and she'd said yes. So here we were.

I'd thought that "yes" meant a truce, but obviously not. Maybe she'd been hoping I wouldn't show. But I had, so what now?

I tugged at my bunches and fought the urge to chew on one, rubbing it across my chin instead.

Hassan let out a breathy laugh. 'Do you want me to pass notes, or something? Is that how this is going to work?'

Darcie rolled her eyes, 'We're fine! It's fine. I'm allowed to be quiet, aren't I? Let's just get on with it.'

Just then, a crowd of boys spilled out the block and started kicking a ball around, automatically falling into teams as soon as their feet hit the playground. Hassan's hand shot to his hair and he smoothed it quickly. He even seemed to sit up straighter, although he looked like he'd rather disappear.

They spotted him.

'Hassan!!!' It was that Luka kid again, the one with the square head and rectangular body. I would totally draw him with tiny little legs spinning beneath. And he was as scruffy as Hassan was smart. 'What *you* doing? A teddy bear's picnic?'

A couple of the others fell into him, laughing as they gathered at the edge of the concrete, kicking the gravel. Hassan glowed pink. One of them wolf whistled – *idiot* – and triggered a second eruption of giggles.

The boy who'd passed me Hassan's note in P.E. last week – Matteo – grabbed Luka by the shirt collar and pulled him back towards the game. 'Let's just play!' He shot Hassan an apologetic smile.

Hassan tossed his acorn on the ground and straightened even more, suddenly grinning. 'We're planning a break-in actually – a *heist* – wanna join us?'

I gasped and tugged Hassan's sleeve. Was this a joke to him? Luka looked from me to him and back. 'She almost looks like you're being serious, mate?' he said, his voice uncertain.

'She just doesn't think you can keep our secret.' Hassan winked at me as I glowered at him.

'We're working the "access points" at the minute . . . have you got the book, Sash?'

'I . . .'

Darcie produced her notebook with a flourish and slapped it into Hassan's hand. He paused to grin at the moving turtle pic on the front and then started flicking through.

'Er . . . no, you're alright, mate,' stuttered Luka. 'I'll leave you to it.' The boys had now turned their grins on him, ready to redirect the constant teasing, especially as Hassan didn't seem too embarrassed. Luka gave into the tugs from Matteo and went back to the game, flashing a confused look at Hassan over his shoulder.

Darcie laughed. Sharing our plan was clearly *hilarious.*

'What?' Hassan raised his hands defensively. 'I wasn't really going to show him. I just wanted him off my back, that's all.'

'Breaking and entering isn't *cool*, you know, Hassan,' Darcie was using a fake cross voice, while stifling little hiccups of laughter. Then she bit her lip. 'Man, that's really what we're doing, isn't it?' Her laughter died out and she stared into her lap, frowning.

I pushed down my annoyance. 'Look, let's make that plan now, it won't take long.' I grabbed the book from Hassan and rooted in my bag for a pen.

'I'm not sure if . . .' Darcie started.

'Yes, you are,' I said. 'Of course you're sure. Here, I'm putting you down for front door security.'

I needed Darcie on board, she made the whole thing make sense. And I needed Hassan to take it seriously.

'But—'

I let out a peal of laughter that sounded like pure hysteria. Even I could tell I seemed desperate.

Darcie looked at me open-mouthed. I didn't know what to say.

'*Darcie*, please. He's being poisoned, remember?'

She threw her hands up. 'OK, OK. Front door security. Get it.'

I couldn't look at her so I turned to Hassan, trying to keep my voice steady. 'Back doors and fire escapes?'

'Aye Aye, Captain.'

My vision blurred as I made notes in the book. *Not a captain. Not a game.* Everything was spiralling out of control.

Someone squeezed my arm and I looked up.

124

'I'm really sorry about your Dadu, Sashi . . . and sorry I couldn't help.'

'Oh! Let's not talk about it.' I blinked away the tears. 'But thank you, for trying. I do appreciate you trying to help, I promise.'

I risked a quick smile, and she half-smiled back.

'Hey,' Hassan was getting to his feet, carefully brushing down his trousers, 'do you two wanna come grab some food before the bell?'

'Are you serious? Sit with you for lunch?' Darcie lit up at Hassan's sheepish look. 'What would that do for your shining reputation?'

'Can't be worse than our teddy bear's picnic!' He huffed a laugh. 'I don't think Luka will give me any more stick now, he's done his worst. And I survived! It's fine.'

They were both acting as if everything was OK.

We set off for the dinner hall arm in arm, just as if our team wasn't really falling apart. As if Ian wasn't being poisoned by some evil fake-keeper. Sunday, I reminded myself. Sunday they would see Ian again. We could find a way to save him. Everything would be better as soon as we were back at the aquarium.

# CHAPTER 13

**HASSAN:** So, we won both the matches yesterday girls, thanks for asking. 6-2, 3-1. I scored both games.

**HASSAN:** Er . . . are we still on for today? What time?

**DARCIE:** They still passed to you then, teddy bear? You're not a total social outcast?

Hassan just sent back an eye-roll emoji and we arranged to meet at the aquarium door. As soon as I had checked in with Ian, I knew everything was going to be OK. Then we'd all got straight on with our tasks.

'Reporting back!' Hassan pulled himself up tall and straight and flicked a crisp salute.

'Repoooooort-ting!' I tried to join in, but I couldn't resist a silly voice. I could not look less like an actual soldier.

We both turned to Darcie.

'Yeah, I'm not doing that,' she laughed.

We'd met back up at the "backstage" door, where we towered above a group of little kids in front of us. The leaflet had said you could learn about feeding and stuff on this behind-the-scenes tour, and it was about to start.

'I don't have much to say,' Hassan started. 'Couldn't find a single other way out.'

'Shh!' Darcie hissed.

The kids were all tugging on the grown-ups' elbows now and starting to mess around, running out of the queue and back, so I didn't think the parents were paying any attention to us. Phew.

Hassan still dropped his voice to a dramatically loud whisper. 'It's like an escape room, or something. Genuinely think the front entrance is it – the rest is sealed shut, I swear.'

'Same here,' I whispered – I was looking at tank access – 'There must be a way in to the tank, just don't know what it is. I'm hoping we'll find out now, though.' I nodded towards the door.

'Sounds good, Sash-a-tron.' Darcie's whisper dropped so low, me and Hassan had to press our ears right up to her face. 'Front door looks like it has a keypad entrance, so we could do with an inside guy. Befriend someone, or follow someone . . . dunno.'

I eyed her, trying to work out if she was actually back on board or just humouring us. It was hard to tell. It sounded like she was playing a spy game.

Then the door opened and my blood ran cold. The keeper creep was standing there, next to some other girl. It was the first time I'd seen him since Ian's message. Since I'd learnt he was hurting him. I wasn't prepared for how violently every cell in my body would react against him. I reached out and grabbed Darcie's fingers. Hassan actually gasped.

'Check it!' he elbowed me sharply in the ribs.

'Ouch! Yes,' I hissed. 'Shh.'

My heart was beating so hard I could feel it in my throat.

The two aquarium employees cast their eyes over us all, and the three of us shuffled as one in the direction of the poisoner.

'We could get evidence,' I whispered to the others. 'We need to be with this guy.' I didn't want to let him out of my sight.

'We've already *got* evidence,' growled Hassan,

narrowing his eyes at the keeper as he patted the phone is his pocket.

*Oh yeah, that.*

'Maybe we should confront him with it?' Hassan took a step forward and I heard myself squeak.

'Easy soldier,' Darcie laid a hand on his back, then slipped it round his elbow. 'Stay on target, we have info to gather. Save it.'

I released the breath that had been strangled in my throat. I wanted to confront this guy, make him pay for hurting Ian, but I couldn't risk Hassan getting out that fake photo.

The girl-aquarium-person beamed at us across the heads of the children. 'I'll take you three, shall I?'

*No.*

'I'm Martha. School project?'

'Yep!' said Darcie. 'Kinda.'

I strained to see over this Martha-person's shoulder and watched in dismay as the curly-haired guy led the little kids through the door. He was already droning away without even looking at them. *Ugh!*

Images from my drawing flashed in my mind. Poison. Ian, trapped. This evil man. Why did he work here?

Why would he hurt the animals? How hadn't anyone noticed what he was doing? My skin was prickling all over and I felt a sickly pull deep in my stomach.

'. . . by the cephalopods really, I mean, that's what our project is mainly on.'

I forced myself to tune back in to Darcie chatting away. Yes. *Stay on target.* Pump for information. I tried to focus: tilt head, look engaged. *This* keeper was pretty friendly and sensible-looking. She had curls too, but hers were a natural afro, scraped back in a tight ponytail. No make-up. She bounced up and down in her bright white trainers, swinging her arms. Not a hint of fake about her.

We moved through the doors and I could see keeper-creep ahead. I pushed round our little group to get a better view of him; his rumpled polo, his slow-blinking eyes. Man, I *hated* him.

'How long have you worked here, Martha? You look young to be a sea life expert.'

My attention flicked back to Hassan. *Seriously?* Was this his idea of getting her on side? *Please.*

'Well, I'm no expert, yet. But everything I'm going to tell you is the latest research on marine life.

And there are some hard facts to face . . .' She was basically reading out an essay. 'Ocean habitats are changing fast due to plastic pollution and over-fishing.'

*Yes, yes, yes . . .*

**FACT: There is more micro plastic in the earth's oceans than stars in the Milky Way.**

Martha was following the other guy into a room full of yet more glass tanks as she talked.

It was nothing like the aquarium outside. This room was hospital bright with those long, flickery lights, instead of all dim and moody with curved glass and floor-to-ceiling tanks. Keeper-creep was bent over a tank, pointing to something inside.

*Sheesh, was he actually feeding something?*

Martha stepped to the side and blocked my view. I strained to see around her, heart beating double-time. She was now holding up what looked like a bag of maggots and laughing and joking with Darcie and Hassan as they hung on her every word. Where was my guy? I was starting to panic. I felt like the only person in the world who knew what he was up to – who could stop him. It was too much.

*There!* He was talking to the kids in front of

131

what looked like a load of seahorses, but also reaching down, all sneaky, into an unlabelled back box. Fishing around for something . . .

My face flushed hot.

*He was going to poison those too!*

I needed to do something – a distraction. I glanced around . . . there was a spanner lying on a desk not too far from me.

*Yes.*

I lunged forward, picked it up and lashed out as hard as I could at the nearest tank. There was a sharp crash, then a shriek and a cry from somewhere. Water soaked my jeans and trainers. I froze. All the panic and heat draining from me instantly.

*What had I done?*

I looked up at my friends, my whole body glued to the spot. Hassan and Martha's mouths hung open as they stared at the floor, but Darcie was looking at me.

Her eyes flicked down to my hand – the spanner seemed to burn hot in my fingers – then back to my face.

My eyes locked on Darcie's, I took one step back and slipped the spanner quietly on to the desk.

# CHAPTER 14

For a millisecond me and Darcie just stood there, looking at each other. Then Darcie broke the spell and looked down at the floor. My eyes followed hers.

*Oh no oh no oh no . . .*

I sank to a crouch on my heels – dozens of silver fish were writhing and gasping and flapping.

*What had I done?*

I scooped up the nearest fish, flinching as its body flicked wetly in my hands.

'I need water!' I looked around, blinking away tears, then half threw it in the nearest tank I could see. I fell on my knees to get another one.

'Stop!' The aquarium girl, Martha, was shouting at me, but I needed to get more fish. Hassan and Darcie were doing the same next to me.

'What the hell did they do?' a male voice boomed. *His.* I froze. *I stopped him. I stopped him. Please.*

'Michael, calm down. It was an accident.'

Martha's face was calm and she was talking in a low voice to the keeper creep. 'Get housekeeping in here. And get those little kids out of here. Right now.' She turned to us. 'You three – you need to stop. Please.'

*What?*

I was standing with another fish now; it wasn't moving as much as the first one had.

'Leave it. *Now.*'

Me, Darcie and Hassan emptied our hands into the water and turned towards Martha.

'There's too much broken glass. I can't risk you getting injured.'

I could hear a wailing sound. 'Just stay over there for a minute, OK? While we clear up. Sashi, is that your name? Calm down for me, all right?'

My ears were wet, and I realised my hands were pressed to them. It was me wailing. I tried to stop.

'Accidents happen, OK? It's not your fault. Look at me.'

*No.*

'Yes.'

I looked up in shock, my cry dying in my throat.

'All of you – I need to sort this out. Please.'

I stared down at the floor where the fish were barely moving at all now, just the odd jerk. One or two had definitely stopped moving completely.

Someone was tugging my hand. 'C'mon Sash-mash, let's get out of her way.'

I let Darcie lead me to the side of the room, but couldn't look at her.

We watched as Martha wheeled over a trolley with an empty looking tank on it and used a net to scoop the fish in. Most of them gradually started moving around the tank, but a few just seemed to float there. I screwed my eyes shut, but a fresh flood of tears streamed out of them and down my cheeks.

A swing door burst open across the room and that curly-haired keeper-creep strutted back in, scowling. He led a group of older people in aquarium uniforms, all dragging mop buckets and carrying bags of cleaning kit. Martha came back over to us.

'OK, time for us to get out of here. I'm going to need to check you all over, make sure you didn't get caught by any splinters of broken glass, OK?'

She was already lifting my arms one at a time and scanning them.

'I'm so sorry . . . I—'

'Shh, it's OK, it's OK.' She was rubbing my shoulder. 'Accidents happen. Did you trip?'

I sobbed and shook my head. I couldn't speak.

'I think she slipped.'

I gasped. Darcie's voice was clear and calm, but when I looked at her, she stared at the floor. Martha pressed her lips together and looked serious.

'Hmm. I just need to talk to my boss before I give you a proper check, OK? So, I'm going to take you all to sit in the staffroom for a minute.'

She ushered us to a room where a few plastic chairs clustered around a filthy plastic table, and left us there.

\*\*\*

'Well, that was dramatic,' laughed Hassan, drumming his fingers on the food-covered tabletop. He was still smiling, so I assumed he hadn't seen what really happened. What I'd done.

I shivered. My jumper was all wet down one side and my jeans were soaked.

'What a jerk the *creeper* is! Yelling like that.'

Darcie looked up at Hassan. 'He was just stressed. I think it's pretty understandable.'

'What are you *talking* about? He's a killer, D.'

Darcie just frowned, and we all sat in silence.

We were in a grimy room. The walls were covered with dog-eared instruction charts on handwashing, and "correct storage procedures" for tubs of various things. There was a bank of lockers, but none of them seem locked; all the doors flapped open, with hoodies and joggers half-falling out of them. Empty plastic water bottles were everywhere, despite the huge display on plastic pollution in the aquarium.

Suddenly, Hassan jumped to his feet.

'Look where we are!' he yelped.

I didn't want to look at anything. 'The *staffroom*, guys. *The lion's den.* If we're going to find out codes and stuff . . . where could be better than here?'

*Codes? Oh, the door code* . . . Darcie looked at me then. She raised her eyebrows and nodded to the corner where there was an ancient-looking desktop computer.

'Great idea, Hassan.' Her voice was flat. 'Me and Sashi will check out the computer.'

I rubbed my hands on my jeans, but just made them wetter, and followed Darcie obediently. She shook the mouse and the screen jumped to life to show a login page with "Martha826" in the username box, but an empty space below for password. I sat down and mechanically started typing in words:

*Octopus.*

*Fish.*

*Plankton.*

No luck.

Darcie pulled up a chair next to me. 'What *the hell* was that?' She was whispering so quietly I could barely hear her, but I looked up to check Hassan wasn't listening anyway. He was opening and shutting drawers on the other side of the room, oblivious.

I turned to Darcie, but her glare was so fierce I couldn't hold it. I tried "aquarium" in the password box. My hands were shaking, but my insides felt like stone.

'He was going to do it again, Darcie. I had to.'

A message popped on to the screen: *"Incorrect username or password."*

'*Who* was going to do *what?*' She was hissing between gritted teeth.

'The . . . the keeper. I saw him. He was putting something in the seahorse tank . . . I . . .'

'Sashi, you *killed* those fish!'

A sob tightened my throat.

'But . . .'

'*What?* To stop him killing *other* fish? That doesn't make any sense!' Darcie pushed her chair back from the desk with a horrible scrape, and I glanced at Hassan again.

'Look, I know it seems bad. It *is* bad. I know, I know.' What was I trying to say? I needed Darcie to understand. 'But . . . he's on some kind of mission and he needs to be stopped.'

I was pleading with her, but Darcie just rolled her eyes and stood up.

'I'm starting to wonder if it's *you* that needs to be stopped, Sashi.'

I opened my mouth, but Hassan called out from across the room. 'Dudes!'

'Don't *call* us that, Hassan,' Darcie snapped. 'You're not hanging out with your "bros" right now. Plus we do actually have names, y'know.'

'Whatever. It's HT-3675. Anyone got a pen?'

Hassan was flipping through a plastic bound folder in a drawer under a rusty microwave.

Darcie shook her head and rolled in her lips 'It's . . .? Huh?"

'The *door code*,' he mouthed. 'Look.' He held up the folder and showed us the "useful info" sheet, in a rubbish font and stained with tea.

'Oh,' she said. 'Of course.' Darcie turned to me with just the slightest hint of a smile and shrugged. 'I guess we got what we came for.'

\*\*\*

Half an hour later we were trailing Martha through the Rainforest Zone. She'd come back for us just as we'd finished copying down and hiding the code, and offered us a personal aquarium tour to "make up for the slip". As if I didn't feel bad enough already.

The air was hot and heavy in this bit. It was creepy and suffocating. Voices echoed everywhere.

I felt like I was walking through fog, but I needed to drag myself out. *I'd stopped him.* That was the bit I mustn't forget. That guy was going to kill more animals and I'd done what I needed to do. None of this was ideal – I didn't exactly think breaking out an octopus was *perfect* – but I had to stay focused.

Before we'd left the staffroom, Martha had given us all a full first-aider's check. Other than one lame scratch on my elbow, we were all fine – but she'd been super careful flushing that out and dressing it. It had given us all a chance to calm down. Hassan had already been fine, but Darcie had flipped from hissing anger to fake cheery mode. Now she was arm-in-arm with Hassan as if nothing had happened.

'So,' Hassan said, 'we're basically being rewarded for smashing stuff up, is that is?' I stumbled, but managed to catch myself. Somehow Hassan managed to say this with a twinkle in his eye that almost made it funny, even though it definitely wasn't.

Martha took him in – wool coat, perfectly combed hair, the swagger of someone who already assumes you'll love them. She looked like she was making up her mind. 'Well, no,' she said with a smile.

He jogged ahead and turned around to walk backwards in front of her, grinning his charming grin. 'So, what would I get if I blew up that shark tunnel? A lifetime entry pass?'

'A jail term, I imagine. So I wouldn't be getting any ideas.'

*Jail term.* Darcie visibly stiffened.

'I'm assuming you don't actually have plans to bomb and destroy my lovely workplace, do you? Or I might take pity on a different three kids for the Martha-special aquarium tour?'

Darcie let out a peal of the most desperately fake-sounding laughter I've ever heard. Like an alarm bell ringing "guilty" at full volume.

'No! Ha ha!' she chimed. *Guilty guilty guilty.* 'We're just here to learn!' She took a deep, shaky breath. 'I'm actually becoming unbelievably obsessed with this project,' she gushed. 'Octopus mating, for example! Insane!' Darcie's best line of defence: go full geek. To be fair, it'd never let her down in the past. She turned to me, then Hassan. 'Did you know that both male and female octopuses die shortly after mating, isn't that sad?'

142

*What?*

I stopped walking. We were next to a tank filled with terrapin and a huge, coiled snake – an anaconda? Weren't they the snakes that squeezed the life out of their prey? Circling round and round their body tighter and tighter until they couldn't breathe. I felt like that was happening to me now.

First the poison, then the fish, now this. All I could see was the picture of Ian's eggs; the grape-like babies in the ocean he needed to get back to. *The whole point.* Then I saw those silver fish floating unnaturally in the new tank. The still ones in the corners of the floor. All of this was for Ian. If octopuses died after mating . . .? How . . .? It just couldn't be true. I couldn't breathe at all – that tight-chested feeling squeezing the air out of me. Darcie was wrong.

'That's not right.' I could barely even hear my own strangled voice, and Darcie was still talking, directing questions at Martha, her face glowing with passion.

'. . . Is this even true? That they remove one of their own arms, that holds their sperm, and just pass it to the female to use it when they feel like it?'

'Props to the octopus, man – that's respectful.'

All three of us turned to Hassan in surprise, as he nodded thoughtfully. He saw us looking and shrugged. 'What?'

I blinked, snapping the distraction away.

'They don't *all* die though, right? And how long ago was Ian brought here?'

'Hang on, hang on a minute.' Martha stopped in front of the poison dart frogs and held up her hands. 'Gosh, you guys have a lot of questions. I'm gonna have to study harder. And who's Ian?'

'The grey ball of octopus jelly that skulks in the tank you have here.'

'Oh!' Martha raised her eyebrows at Hassan, then turned to me. '*Ian?* Right, OK. Well, our octopus is a juvenile, Sashi, he's not reached maturity yet, so he won't have mated.' I started shaking my head, but Martha continued. 'As for *reproduction.* You're right, Darcie, they do die after mating. And not a whole lot is known about the rest – we're still finding out information and there are new theories all the time. They're certainly unconventional though, and different sub-species have different behaviours. I know with the giant Pacific octopus . . .'

**FACT: I didn't want to know.**

Martha carried on talking but her words faded to a buzz. It couldn't be true. I'd seen it. I'd drawn it. Ian's left-behind babies. How would I have known what octopus eggs even *looked* like if Ian hadn't shown me? Tears filled my eyes. I knew it was real. Ian's messages were the only thing that made sense, everything else was confusion. The hum of people closed in on me, as dead fish filled my mind again – then the look in Darcie's eyes when she saw the spanner.

It couldn't have all been for nothing. I refused to believe it.

# CHAPTER 15

I couldn't get out of bed. I didn't want to go to school. I didn't want to ever take my head out from under this pillow. I didn't want to *think*, ever again. But when I closed my eyes all I could see were tentacles and suckers and bulging octopus eyes pleading with me. Ian wanted me to understand, but I didn't understand anything any more. Why did I ever even think I could save him?

'Sashi, love? Are you in there? It's 7:20.'

I buried my head deeper. Darcie's face when she said I needed stopping. Silver flashes of fish on the floor. Hassan laughing like it was all a joke. The images kept spinning in front of me.

'Sashi?'

Mum normally left me to get ready for school by myself. I didn't think she'd even notice I wasn't up. But there you go, she noticed.

I gave a vague grunt and waited to see if she'd go away.

The rest of the tour yesterday had been a blur. It was like I was looking in from the outside as Hassan and Darcie had a whale of a time with that Martha – Ms Ocean Genius' newest cheerleaders, competing with each other to make her laugh. Maybe it had paid off . . . I guess. Their faces as Martha pushed on that invisible door! It was disguised as part of a terrible seascape mural. 'Hassan!' Darcie had hissed, swinging her arms to display the now-obvious opening he'd missed on his door patrol. Then some stairs had led us to a secret platform overlooking a row of tanks. And there, below us: Ian. Darcie and Hassan had bounced with glee, although Darcie wouldn't even look at *me*.

I should be thrilled – we'd got everything we'd wanted – the door code, a way into his tank and, despite everything that had happened, Darcie still *seemed* to be following the plan – so why did everything feel so hopeless?

My door clicked open as Mum let herself in. I growled from my head-buried position and yanked the pillow closer round my face as soft footsteps

147

crossed the room – I couldn't face a pep talk. But instead, a rush of cool air hit my side as the duvet lifted, then the mattress dipped suddenly, nearly rolling me out, as Mum climbed in next to me.

I edged the pillow up to see, and Mum just settled on her back, so I lay beside her and let her take my hand.

'What's going on with you, Sashi, my darling? You've not been yourself for weeks now. Can we talk about it?'

I rolled over and faced the wall and felt Mum roll on her side behind me. She rested her chin on my shoulder. I was frozen.

'OK,' she said.

We lay there for a moment. Mum started stroking my hair like she used to when I was about seven. Picking up strands and tucking them, then running a finger around the outside of my ear. It was almost unbearable. Ears are pretty sensitive.

Mum was all right, really. I knew she meant well. When I was little, I used to think she was too busy for me because she never wanted to play. Of course, she did sometimes, but mostly she had jobs to do, or spent all day just staring at her phone.

When it was a Dadu-day he was all about me –
100%. I could see now how lucky I was to have had
that. We used to build things . . . everything . . . Lego,
dens, marble runs that filled the room and complex
paper airplanes. He always wanted to explain the
mechanics of them, but I just drew passengers in the
windows. Cardboard box houses were his speciality:
curtains on the windows, letter boxes, even super-
fancy door knockers with lions on.

Dadu once made a cardboard igloo out of triangles.
He measured it all out and cut it to some mysterious
pattern, scribbling numbers in his notepad and
frowning. Then, when he started taping them, they
slotted together in this amazing dome. It was magic.
We'd filled it with duvets and soft toys, and I'd been
heartbroken weeks later when Mum and Dad said it
had to go in the recycling.

My Dadu-days were always a big flurry of activity
in the mornings, then we'd watch TV all afternoon . . .
he would fall asleep with an arm around me and
I would snuggle into his belly and hope he didn't
wake up and turn CBeebies off. Mum would never
let me watch that much TV.

Now I was older, though, at least Mum knew not to ask questions when I was feeling sad. And Dadu wasn't here any more.

'Can I trust you with a secret, Sashi?'

That pulled me out of my thoughts. Mum pushed herself up on her elbow and looked down on me.

I wiped my eyes and nodded. 'Course, Mum.' It wouldn't be a proper secret.

'I don't want your dad to get upset, he's only trying to protect us. You must understand that. Everything he does, is because he's putting you first.'

*Oh. Perhaps this* was *going to be a real secret.*

'And I do agree with him as far as you're concerned – I know you don't get it now, but you will. He's right about that. But it's different for us . . .'

What was she talking about? I rolled on to my back to see her properly.

'Did I tell you the story of when your father and I first got together?'

My eyes flicked to my bedside clock: 7:27. Had she forgotten about school? Fine by me.

'Is this the secret, Mum?'

'He really is the funniest man I've ever met,

your father. The first month we were together I think I laughed more than in my entire life up until that point. That's a pretty good recommendation for a boyfriend, isn't it?'

*Boyfriend? Ew.*

'You'd think anybody would be happy to hear their daughter say that. I'd found this wonderful, kind, beautiful, hilarious man—'

'Are you sure you're talking about Dad?' I giggled.

'Don't be smart, Sashi.'

This was weird. Mum usually sounded irritated by Dad. I always kind of assumed she thought he was an idiot.

'Do you still think that stuff, Mum?'

'What stuff?'

'That he's funny, and kind and things?'

'YES, yes. Always. But my point now, Sashi, is that my parents, your grandparents—'

'Nanny Carol and Grandad Paul?' We rarely saw them – just a day trip around Christmas, and maybe once over summer. They always gave me ridiculous girly gifts as though I were still five.

'Exactly. Well, they didn't care one bit about how

lovely he was. They didn't want a thing to do with him. I suppose they thought I'd drop him instantly, rather than dare risk their disapproval. It wasn't until I was pregnant with you that they finally accepted we were together, really.'

'Why? Did they not get his sense of humour?' I grinned.

'Oh, Sashi, they just . . . Well, they were a different generation, and quite stuck in their ways. They wanted me to marry a nice Protestant boy from our church, I imagine.'

*Oh.*

'Oh, Sash.' She sat up and tugged me on to her lap and touched my cheek. 'Listen to me, this isn't about them at all. My point is: your *Dadu.* Your Dadu . . .' Her face kind of crumpled when she said his name, and my insides did the same. 'Your dad's Mum was long gone, but when my parents kicked me out, your Dadu . . . well, he threw his arms wide and made his family my family – and I've not looked back. He means the world to me, Sashi . . . the world.'

I struggled to get down from her lap. How was this suddenly about Dadu? I scooted back against the wall and pulled my knees to my chest.

It was *me* that had the special relationship with him. I was his "Little Fish", wasn't I? I was the one who always made him smile, that he built cardboard houses for, that he always wanted to sit next to when we ate, saying, "I've saved a space for my special girl" and patting the seat next to him.

'I'm still visiting him every week, my angel. He still doesn't know who I am. He doesn't want me there, or *says* he doesn't, but I'm not going to stop. I thought you'd want to know that. Your dad doesn't need to know.'

So *that* was the secret.

Tears flooded down my face.

'Mum, I don't want to go to school today.'

Mum sighed. 'OK, sunshine. We all need some time sometimes. I'll call the office. Stay in bed for now.'

I lay down and pulled the pillow back over my head, breathing in the foggy smell of my own breath.

'Right,' said Mum. I knew she was waiting, hoping I would say something about Dadu, but I pulled the pillow down tighter. 'I'll leave you to it, my love.' And the door clicked closed.

\* \* \*

A few hours later I was still in my room. Trapped. I didn't want to be in bed any more, but I didn't want to go downstairs either, in case Mum started talking about Dadu again.

I knew it was silly to be jealous of Mum's relationship with him, but I still wanted to delete the whole conversation. She'd told me nothing new anyway; Dadu had always been kind. If I were in trouble with Mum and Dad, he'd sneak me sweets and tell me that all good children are naughty sometimes. If my school reports said I didn't concentrate, he told me tales of how he was always late for school back in Calcutta – he used to beg his driver to detour on the way in, so he could feed biscuits to the crows and stray dogs at Victoria Memorial. He had so many stories like that. I missed curling up with him and hearing all about his childhood, and imagining him in India. I knew all the names of his friends back there, he always told me how much they would love me when we visited, but we'd never gone.

Now my face was all pillow creased and sticky, so I dragged myself to the bathroom and scrubbed it but I still looked blotchier than Ian. I splashed again with extra icy water then held the towel to my face for a minute. That would do.

Mum was humming somewhere when I went down, so I dived straight into the kitchen and rooted in the cupboard for some cereal.

'Sashi!' She appeared at the door with a huge smile. 'You're down, great. Do you want to come shopping?'

'Like, food shopping? To the supermarket?'

'No! I thought we could have a girls' day! Go to that comic-book shop you like, have a mooch. I dunno, what do you like these days? Do you want to look at clothes?'

'Er, don't you have work stuff?' She worked supply as an art teacher and seemed to spend every spare minute planning lessons.

'It can wait. What do you think? Eat some breakfast, then we can go and make something of the day . . .?'

'OK, yeah.' Maybe our "chat" was truly over. 'The comic shop would be great.'

It was only a ten-minute walk from our house, it was silly how little we came. We held hands as we weaved through the backstreets into town. It was so quiet in the middle of the day – not nearly so many bikes chained to fences, ready to trip you up. Mum gazed in all the windows; everyone else's house looked unbelievably fancy inside. I preferred it when the neat little terraced homes gave way to cafés and restaurants and I could breathe in the fumes of all the lunches being prepared – stepping from India, to Italy, to Thailand, just in smells.

The comic shop was tucked down a quiet street next to a tattoo parlour. We pushed open the door and let the bell ring into the silence. We were the only customers. I shot an awkward smile to the guy at the till, but he perched on his stool without looking up, engrossed in something that looked 90% inked in black.

After five minutes of browsing I saw a graphic novel with a huge alien on the front clearly based on an octopus – suckered arms writhing aggressively all over the cover in streaks of black and red.

A wave of exhaustion washed over me and I sank on to a low stepladder in the corner of the shop. *Ian.* For a few short hours, I'd almost managed to forget both those poor dead fish *and* Martha's bombshell. She'd said Ian was a "juvenile". He hadn't even mated, so how could he have babies waiting for him at home? What did it all mean?

I flicked through the comic, without really looking. It all seemed a bit violent and I wasn't in the mood. Then a caption caught my eye.

*What did that say?*

I skimmed back through the book trying to find it again. *There.* The picture was horrible – the tentacled alien guy was saluting in the middle of the page, surrounded by what I could only imagine were his fallen enemies in various states of destruction. But, for once, I wasn't interested in the picture. There it was, at the top:

### Errol's Vision Of The Future.

I slammed the book shut without seeing any more of this Errol-alien's dreams. *That was it.* That must have been what Ian was showing me. Not the babies waiting back home, but the babies in his *future* that he would never have, because he was trapped in a stupid tank! It all made sense. Ian was begging me to save his vision of the future!

I sat with the book in my lap, letting the new knowledge filter in. So, the plan was back on!

And here I was on a stool in a comic shop, wasting time, while Ian was slowly being poisoned. Ian still needed me, but I still needed help. And I had no idea where I stood with Darcie and Hassan.

I looked across to where Mum was humming as she ran her fingers carelessly over the spines. Could I tell Mum about Ian? She would know what to do and she'd be behind us in principle, I knew she would – it was about animal welfare, wasn't it?

Now we had the door code and a way into the tank, there weren't too many barriers left . . . just how to transport him and set him free. When to do it. *If I had a team.* But, if Mum could help us, we'd be able to do it properly. And we'd all know for certain we were doing the right thing.

'Look, this one looks good!' Mum came over, her face stuck in the middle of a terrible, cheesy-looking, superhero comic about some girl gang taking over the world. The drawings were total Marvel rip-offs.

The walls of the shop were covered with huge superhero posters to draw in the tourists, but dig a bit deeper and there were all sorts of strange, cool stories here.

'Yeah, Mum, looks great. Think I've got one a bit like that already, though.'

'Oh, OK.' She clapped it closed. 'What have you got there? Oh! Another octopus?'

'Yeah. Y'know, I wanted to talk to you about the one at the aquarium actually . . .' I shifted on the stool.

'Ah, your school project! It certainly sounded interesting from what Darcie was saying. I couldn't stop your dad talking about them after he read that book too – the whole world is octopus obsessed! Are you doing some drawings to go with it? Great subject matter, all that movement . . .'

'Uh, well the thing is, my drawings are coming from . . .' *How to say this?* 'Well, when I look at him, they just sort of . . . come out. And, well—'

'Oh, you *are* feeling inspired. I think this project is great for you, darling.' Mum stroked my hair and leant down to kiss my head. 'Getting you into science. Inspiring your art. Great for your friendships with Darcie *and* Hassan – it's so nice to see the two of you together again, you've been friends for so many years.'

The thought of great friendships made me crumble inside.

'Come here, my lovely.' Mum's magic sensors were working again. She reached out for me to stand up and I did. She pulled me into a hug and I leant into it, absorbing all the comfort I could get, explanation abandoned.

*The project's great for my friendship with Darcie! As if!* I replayed Darcie's words – "maybe it's you that needs stopping". It was pushing us further apart than we'd ever been. And just when I needed her the most.

# CHAPTER 16

*Buzz Buzz.*

The vibration of my phone travelled across the surface of the breakfast table.

I glanced up at Dad, but he was too hypnotised by his own screen to notice. Mum was upstairs getting ready for work. My breath was suddenly really shallow. I'd not heard from Darcie since the disaster at the aquarium. I shoved a spoonful of muesli in my mouth and chewed.

Swipe.

**DARCIE:** Sash-a-lac, babe. Don't take this the wrong way, but I think you may have made a mistake about Michael.

**ME:** OK. Who's Michael?

**DARCIE:** Y'know, the keeper at the aquarium? You thought he was poisoning Ian?

I nearly spat out my cereal.

*"Thought"?* It was bad enough she knew I'd smashed the tank on purpose. Was she going to start questioning the whole reason I'd done it? On a group chat?

**HASSAN:** That fake-curly-haired octopus-i-cidal maniac??!

Ah, Hassan. If Darcie hadn't been in the middle of calling me a liar, I could take some time to reflect on just how cool he was being. But no.

**ME:** He IS poisoning Ian!

I paused. My thumbs hovering over the screen. Was I going to dig in deeper on that fake photo? Yes.

**ME:** I sent you proof, remember? I saw him do it!

I picked up my spoon again and took another mouthful, chewing thoughtfully. She was going to tell Hassan about the spanner, I knew she was. I couldn't lose Hassan – I already felt like I was losing Darcie.

But she'd stood up for me, hadn't she? To Martha? I thought she'd at least ask why I'd skipped school yesterday. When my phone had buzzed, I'd assumed it was about that. Also, what's with calling him "Michael"?

**DARCIE:** I know what you think you saw, I just think there's been a misunderstanding. Anyway — thought we could have an emergency juice bar sesh?

Misunderstanding?? *Think* I saw? Or was this really about what *she* saw? About the fish?

**HASSAN:** Juice bar?

**DARCIE:** You'll like it, they have protein shakes.

**HASSAN:** Huh? Are you laughing at me again?

**DARCIE:** Hey, sorry. Bad joke. Hope you can come.

I sent Hassan directions, then shoved together the world's most rubbish packed lunch before mumbling something to Dad about an early homework club.

\*\*\*

It didn't take long to power into town, and I skidded my bike to a stop in the usual spot before pushing through the heavy door into the sweet-smelling fug of the juice bar.

Our usual Kind Lady was still behind the counter. How strange that the world had stayed the same, while everything in my life seemed so different. Last time I'd been here had been just after the row with Dad. Now I was a photo-faker, a fish-killer and an octopus thief-in-waiting. Would Kind Lady be able to tell?

But she smiled at me, kid-sized cup ready in her hand.

'Ah, Sashi, you're back. Would you like to browse, or should I start you up a Blueberry Blitz?'

'Y'know, maybe I'll try something new today.' I couldn't sit and drink the same old drink as though I were the same old me. I just wasn't.

'You should have one of these, Sash, they're *amazing*.'

Hassan emerged from the back of the shop, holding up a giant cup of some hideous-looking neon green thing, his eyes bright.

'Oh,' Kind Lady tilted her head with a smile. 'This young gentleman is with you, is he? I would have given him discount!'

'Er . . . looks great?' I gave him my biggest smile.

'It's a "Green Zinger Power". Go on, get one.'

The juice lady turned to look at me, one eyebrow raised.

'Yeah? Er . . . one of those.' I nodded towards it and pulled a face – we shared a deeply doubtful look before she disappeared to mix it, chuckling to herself. Mental note: bring my parents here so they leave a big tip.

Hassan concentrated on sucking.

I shoulder bumped him. 'You should be flattered, you know.'

164

He looked up. 'That you chose the same juice as me?'

'No, you doofus!' I slapped him weakly. 'The text. "Protein shakes" or whatever. That Darcie teases you.'

Better to focus on this than risk him asking about my "misunderstanding".

But all the sparkle fell from his face and his cheeks deflated. 'Oh, right. Really? Yeah, it's super flattering when someone's constantly telling you what a meathead loser you are.'

So much for water-off-a-chick's-back, or whatever the saying was.

'She would never tease you to be cruel, OK? But she teases me – or used to – constantly. Like, every single second. It's a sign of affection, I promise.'

'Right. You're very forgiving of her, Sashi. She's not perfect. You shouldn't let her boss you round so much.'

I shook my head. *I was hoping* she *would be very forgiving of* me. 'I promise she'll be feeling terrible now she knows you're hurt. 100% guaranteed.'

'Why *wouldn't* I get hurt? You two think I don't feel anything!'

'That's not true!'

*Is it?*

Kind Lady brought over my green juice at just that second, giving me a chance to think what to say next. It wasn't that I didn't think he cared what anyone thought . . .

'It's just . . . you know . . . why would you care what we think? Look at you!'

'What does *that* mean?'

'Oh, you know. Half the girls at school follow you around. You're friends with literally anyone you want to be. The teachers can't get enough of you. Why would you be interested in a pair of fringe nobodies like me and Darcie? I know you're embarrassed of us.'

Hassan put down his juice and locked my gaze with his clear brown eyes, his expression serious. 'I'm not, I promise.' He smiled a weak half-smile. 'I just don't want to give losers like Luka ammunition – he gets so boring and I can't be bothered to deal with it. I shouldn't just let it slide though.' He shrugged. 'Anyway, you're not nobodies.'

I couldn't stop a warm glow flowing through me.

'Darcie's top of the class!' he continued. 'At everything, in every subject. And she's funny too . . .'

The glow drained out of me as quickly as it had flooded in. *Of course.* '. . . everyone knows that.'

'Everyone knows what?' Darcie plonked down a classic Blueberry Blitz on the table and I looked at it enviously as I took a slurp of my weird green juice. Hassan had turned as pink as a plum, but his face was entirely unmoving. Darcie just looked distracted as she unwound her scarf and settled into the booth.

'How "funny" *you* are, Darcie.' Maybe she'd finally admit it: she belonged in the in-crowd with Hassan, and not with a liability like me.

Hassan let out a bark of awkward laughter, but Darcie just guffawed heartily as she shoved her scarf and gloves in her bag.

'Nice one!' Then she turned to Hassan. 'Mate, I'm so sorry I keep being such a cow to you. I don't know why I do it, honestly. I've just been stressed out. And intimidated by your perfection, of course!' She winked at him, and they both laughed. 'Will you forgive me?'

'You've introduced me to Green Zinger Power Juice, so I reckon we're even.'

'Seriously? That looks like a punishment. What even is that? Can I try it?'

She took a sip.

Watching Darcie in charm-mode, I felt drawn back to the familiar warm cocoon of our friendship. I could settle back into this happy place and bed down here for ever. Then my blood ran cold as I remembered the fish, her face, the entire reason we were here . . .

Darcie was giggling and pulling a face at the gross drink, then she straightened up and turned to face me. *This was it.*

'Anyway,' she said, 'we should focus before we run out of time. We need an emergency meeting about Michael.'

*Or did she mean "about Sashi"? She was going to tell Hassan – how could she not?*

I had a really horrible feeling about this.

*"Emergency meeting".*

I tried to push down the dread. 'Do we really?' I asked. My voice sounded sulky, but I couldn't help it. 'And since when are we calling him "Michael"?'

A flicker passed over Darcie's face. Annoyance? Suspicion? Concern? I couldn't tell.

'Yeah, let's get down to business.' Hassan pushed his drink to one side and leant his arms on the table, his whole body tipping forwards. 'What's all this about?'

'Right, well, don't be mad at me, OK? But we just learnt so much with Martha at the weekend, I wanted to go back. She said we could anytime, to finish the backstage tour that got, y'know,' her eyes flicked up at me, 'er . . . cancelled.' She was spinning her cup around in her long fingers, if she wasn't careful it was going to Blueberry Blitz all over the table.

I leant back into the cushions; eyes scrunched closed.

*'Anyway,* so I thought we could go after school yesterday, but then you were off, Sashi, and I tried to find you, Hassan, but you were in basketball I think?'

'Yeah, Mondays.'

'So, I just went by myself. And Martha showed me round backstage properly. It's *a-mazing* guys.'

Just the thought of that backstage area made my face burn.

'They do so much conservation work there. They rescue loads of creatures that wouldn't survive without them. They breed animals that are struggling in the wild. They showed me so much stuff.'

**FACT: The common octopus is NOT endangered OR threatened.**

Still, it did sound good, I had to admit it. Why did Darcie make everything so confusing?

'Who's "they"?' Hassan genuinely looked like he hadn't guessed yet.

'Well, that's my point. Martha and Michael both showed me round. It's really quiet on Mondays. They're both so nice.'

*Nice?*

' – they're on the same Marine Biology course at the university and they both really care about the creatures there. If they were going to poison anyone it would be the visitors!'

Keeper-creep had totally sucked her in!

'Hang on a minute,' Hassan squeaked forwards on the plastic-y seat. 'Sashi saw him put poison on the food. She has a *photo.*' He picked up his phone and started scrolling back through our chat stream to find it.

Darcie wasn't looking at Hassan though, she was looking at me.

'Look, found it! Here's the pic.' Then Hassan looked

up open-mouthed. 'Are you saying Sashi made the whole thing up?'

His question hung in the air for an eternity.

'No, of course not. But . . . I have done a bit of research on that label . . .'

Every hair on my body was standing up and the roof of my mouth was dry. I picked up my drink, took a sip and nearly gagged. *Seriously? What was in this?*

'. . . And it's rat poison. The kind you buy at B&Q and use in your garage.'

*Just say it if you're going to say it. I dare you.*

'So . . .' Darcie paused. She looked right at me, then away. 'They could very well have had it around if there was a mouse problem in the aquarium. Maybe the pot was next to something for Ian and it just *looked* like Michael put his hand in this one. It's very dark in there – it's easy to make a mistake.' Darcie threw me a half-smile. I relaxed, but then she started speaking again.

'Sashi, are *you* going to tell him, or am *I*?'

My fingers burned as if Darcie's eyes were still resting on the spanner in my hands.

'I . . .'

I shook my head so slightly I'm amazed she noticed.

'Tell me *what?*'

Eyes still locked on mine, Darcie turned her head to Hassan, shifting her gaze at the very last second.

I was shaking my head more now, but neither of them noticed.

'Sashi thought Michael was poisoning the seahorses backstage at the weekend, but it turned out there was no evidence for that, either.'

I waited. She didn't seem about to say anything else. 'I don't get it,' Hassan threw his phone down on the table and it skid to a stop in a puddle of melted ice so he picked it up again instantly and wiped it with a serviette. 'If keeper-creep—'

'Michael,' interjected Darcie.

'Whatever . . . if he's not poisoning, then Ian's not in any danger, right?'

I sat up straight, my heart beating so hard I could feel it in my throat.

'*Free Ian*, remember?' Our chant on the beach seemed a million years ago. 'That was the plan before we knew anything about . . . Michael. He needs to get back home.' Tears filled my eyes. 'To be free.' To *live the future he dreams of.*

Darcie finally put her cup down and reached out to me, she tried to take my hand but I snatched my fingers away and sat on them. She sighed. 'Sashi, that's the thing. This has been fun, but I think Ian is in the best place for him. Those guys take really good care of him – I think he's happy there. Listen, this is what we can—'

'You don't know anything about how he feels!' I was yelling, desperately trying to pull the tears back into my eyes, but I knew they were going to overflow whether I liked it or not. I slapped my palms on the bench in frustration. 'You don't know anything about him. How can you say where he'd be happy?'

'C'mon Sashi, can *you?*'

'Yes!' I stood up and screamed it at her.

'OK, OK, sit down.' She was looking to Hassan now, no doubt for backup.

*Ugh!* I started picking up my coat and gloves. I should have known Darcie would never do this – breaking rules wasn't exactly her strong suit. Hassan was just staring at the tabletop, arms still folded, like he was hoping it would swallow him up – pathetic! Then he turned to me and put a hand on my shoulder.

I wanted to push him off but waited for him to say whatever annoying thing he wanted to say.

'Sashi.' *At least he used my full name for once.* 'If you still want to do this, we *can* still do this, OK? If it's that important to you.'

He was giving me that look again, the serious one, that almost looked like caring. I burst into tears and he pulled me into a hug, and I let him. Darcie gave an exasperated sigh. I pulled away from Hassan and wiped my nose on my sleeve.

'WHAT?' I turned to her.

'Oh, Sashi, just because you can do it doesn't mean you *should.*' She flashed Hassan a withering look. 'Can't you just . . . *stop?*'

'No,' I sniffed and held my head high. 'I won't. Maybe you should keep your promises. How about that?'

Darcie got up too and put her coat back on.

'I'm out, Sash-a-lac. I'm so sorry, I just can't be part of it. I don't think it's right. And I really hope you both see that too.'

She smiled sadly and walked out of the juice bar.

# CHAPTER 17

That was the longest day I'd spent at school, ever. It had been endless and horrible. Now I was finally back home but I couldn't get my stupid key in the lock. *Go. IN.* There. I mashed the full length of my body against our front door, turned the key and fell into the house. Stupid door.

I crumpled to the mat and cried into my knees; loud, shaky, ugly sobs. All the tears I'd been holding in for every single class of the day.

It had been impossible to avoid Darcie, and she had apparently found it impossible not to give me these awful puppy-eyed pleading looks every time she saw me. Which was every five minutes. I didn't get it. She'd ignored me for a week for teasing her about Hassan, but now she knew I was a killer and a liar she still wanted to be friends? I guessed she knew how much of a betrayal it was ditching the team like that!

I wanted to scream at her for not trusting me, but also burst into tears and hug her.

So, I just had to hold it all in and get as far away from her as possible. Which is what I'd been doing all day. Holding it in, running away. Hold and run. Hold and run.

There are only so many places to run. Especially when you're stuck in a lesson. I'd never doodled so hard in my life. I now also know every bit of graffiti on the door of every loo – including about fifty declarations of love for Hassan! *Please!* I also added my own Sharpie contribution of an octopus capturing an unnamed blond girl, King Kong style.

Now I was sitting on the scratchy doormat, finally by myself. Mum was working today, so the house was empty. My phone buzzed in my bag again. It would be Darcie telling me what a liar I was.

Or Hassan, backing out of the plan. I couldn't look.

I wiped my eyes and peeled myself off the mat to go on a chocolate hunt. There was an ancient KitKat at the back of a kitchen cupboard. I ate it in silence but didn't feel any better. *Was* I making the whole thing up?

Darcie was right about the rat poison – the photo was fake. I knew she knew it; I could tell by that look she'd given me. It was true I hadn't *actually* seen keeper-creep put it in the tank. It was a white lie, so they could believe me. *But, was it really true? Or could he be nice as Darcie said?*

The chocolate bar swished like molten lava in my tummy and more tears stung my eyes.

I dragged myself upstairs and took down my sketchbook from the top my wardrobe. There was Ian. Just seeing him sent a bolt of energy through me. My fingers tingled on the book like pins and needles and a shiver ran over my skin. That feeling – back when I'd woken up to find my amazing dream had been real! My own pen having drawn thoughts that were not my own: Ian's stolen future. Images I'd never seen before. Those eggs strung like grapes. Knowledge I just didn't have.

It was real. I knew it was real.

I closed my eyes and imagined looking into Ian's real eyes, instead of pen and ink ones. You could feel his intelligence, his longing. How awful it must be to have all those thoughts, those emotions, to want to communicate, when all you can do is reach out an arm and touch someone. To be so intelligent and so loving, but trapped.

I thought of Martha and all her grand ideas of caring for him, and felt even worse.

Poor Ian! Trapped in a home by people who think they know what's best for you – who say they're caring for you and assume you're happy – but don't bother spending the time with you to work out what you really want. No one to be able to see the suffering behind those eyes.

*Just like Dadu.*

The thought snuck unwanted into my brain and pushed it down, hard.

I was crying again and a tear fell on the drawing, smudging a line.

I needed to see Dadu. I closed my eyes and shook my head. *No!* I needed to see *Ian.*

What time was it? The aquarium was still open for another hour. If Darcie could go after school, why couldn't I?

I ran downstairs, left a note on the dining table, and

pulled on my coat, absentmindedly scanning my phone messages, forgetting I'd been avoiding them.

**HASSAN:** Sash, you ok?

**HASSAN:** Worried about you. Message me.

**HASSAN:** You know I'm here for you. Let me know what I can do.

**HASSAN:** Still on for Project Free Ian. Just so you know.

So smooth. Always trying to calm the waters. At least he wasn't backing out.

There was a similar stream from Darcie. She wasn't calling me a liar as I'd thought she would, she was "checking I was OK". What if she actually meant it? If I could go to her house right now and make up? Call off the project. Go back to how things were?

I got on my bike, rolled to the end of the path and paused, her messages spinning in my head. But I couldn't. I couldn't stop this now anyway. Ian needed me. I turned right, away from Darcie's house and towards the seafront. I was heading for the aquarium but when I got there, my feet just kept pedalling. I pushed upwards, with the wind hitting me sideways. Up the coast road to the top of the cliffs. I didn't know where I was going or what I would do next.

# CHAPTER 18

I glanced up at the dark sky as I pedalled along the cliffside – winter storm season was here and it looked like one was coming. But instead of making me feel gloomier, the sight of the racing clouds sent an unexpected thrill of excitement through me. The higher I got, the less sad I felt. My thighs burned with the effort, but this was what I needed . . . some air, some time to think.

I cycled hard, all the way to the top of the coast road, until I was so high the seagulls were screeching round my head and my breath ripped through my throat in hot slices. Then I walked my bike over to the cliff path to look out to sea.

The wind was even fiercer up here, it stung my cheeks and threatened to push me off my feet. And the sea that had been as still as silk not so long ago was bucking up in white-capped angry looking waves. I imagined Ian out there, tossed back and forth, thrown around from wave to wave and laughed. I could barely hear my own voice, the sound of the wind was so loud.

No wonder he was bored in that tiny little tank, living that still, placid life if this was what he wanted! The freedom of this great wild ocean, compared to that. What could be more different?

But something made me stop. Something Hassan had said once about cold seas. Would he really like it here? In these cold English waters? In those vicious, smashing waves? How could I fix this? I was still tingling all over from the exhilaration of the ride and I would not accept defeat. I *had* to make this work.

A white shape loomed into my vision, breaking into my thoughts as it pushed into the storm. A chunky white arrow pointing out across the sea. *This way,* it said. The ferry. We'd got it once for a long weekend in France, busing to the port just down the road.

*Yes.*

*That was it!*

I jumped back on my bike and set off down the hill, picking up speed until I was flying. My face was numb within seconds and all I could hear was the whistling in my ears. I'd never cycled this fast before. My bike was shaking so much, I was definitely not quite in control. A car thundered past, buffeting me slightly to the side, and I gripped the handlebars tighter.

'Whoo-hoooooooooooooooooooo!!' I whooped as loud as I could, throwing my head back to send my battle cry into the sky.

It didn't matter about the poison.

It didn't matter that Ian was trapped in a half-life.

It didn't matter that Darcie had backed out of our team.

This was *my* project now; I was in charge . . . and I knew what I needed to do.

Why was I always looking to Darcie? Project Free Ian was my idea from the start, but the first thing I'd done had been to hand the whole thing over to her. It was time to do something for myself. She was free, she could hang out with whichever cool kids she wanted. I wasn't her sidekick! This was going to be *my* thing and I was going to do it without her. It was all for the best.

Ian could grow up in the wild. Find his mate and have his babies if that's what he wanted. Even if that did mean he would die – I shook off the chill that threatened – at least he would be free. I nodded to myself in the cold wind as my bike hurtled down the hill. It was his decision to make. He'd spoken to *me*, not Darcie, and this was our one chance. He could die with his new family, not alone all by himself.

I could feel unwanted thoughts – about Dadu – bubbling to the surface again and I pushed them down. *Concentrate.* I needed to plan.

I couldn't expect Ian to swim all the way to warmer waters. I would take him there myself.

I was twelve. I could do this. How hard could it be? That ferry . . . then a train, maybe . . .? Yes. I needed to think *bigger.*

**FACT: The biggest octopus can measure six metres from arm tip to arm tip – longer than the height of a fully grown adult giraffe!**

My bike rattled and slowed as the road evened out, and I peddled until I reached our normal beach. I was still going to need help. I pulled up and got out my phone.

**ME:** Can you meet at the beach? Plan update.

I dumped my bike on the beach and laid down next to it on the stones.

We also needed to set a date.

'Seriously? The *Mediterranean*?'

Hassan picked up another stone and hurled it overarm into the sea, where it hit the top of a huge wave, just as it crashed down. His hair had blown completely out of place and the wind was tugging at his clothes. His questions were starting to get a bit annoying.

'Yes! The Mediterranean! It's a super warm sea, isn't it? Wasn't it you who said Ian needed warmer water?'

'Well, I understand *why* you want to do it. I just don't understand *how*.'

'C'mon, it's going to be epic. And I can do it.' I bashed him in the shoulder, making him sway. 'I can! I don't need you to come with me, Hassan. I can do it by myself. We're going on an adventure, me and Ian! How hard can it be, anyway? A ferry to France, there must be a train down to the south coast, then just plop him in the nice warm waters! Just imagine – an octopus on a train!'

I threw my arms above my head and it felt like the wind was going to lift me off my feet. I ran down the beach with my mouth open, tasting the salty spray on my tongue. It was starting to get dark. I ran back to Hassan laughing, my mouth still hanging open.

Hassan laughed too. 'Sashi, you've gone wild. Are you turning into a mer-person? Are you going to set yourself free in the sea too?'

'YES!' I dashed towards the foam as if to dive in, but Hassan grabbed my hand.

'I don't trust you!' he shouted. 'I think you might actually do it, and it's freezing!'

I shivered, suddenly cold to the core. It *was* freezing now the sun had gone down. My bones were made of ice.

Hassan tugged at my hand. 'C'mon, we should get home, it's late.' He paused. 'And maybe you're right about warmer seas. You couldn't chuck the poor guy out into this!' He nodded at the churning, icy-looking English Channel.

There were days in the summer when it looked as clear as crystal and so turquoise, like a holiday advert. But not today, not in a million years. It was hard to imagine anything but a sea monster surviving in the water in front of us now.

'But it's not *just* about how you get there. It can't be very safe, y'know . . .'

*Right.* He just couldn't be bothered to work out a route. So lazy! We'd got the door code, hadn't we? Found the way into Ian's tank? All the things we'd thought were impossible . . . We could find a way to do this too.

'We get the bus by ourselves all the time, don't we?' I scowled. 'How different is it to get a ferry?' I started walking faster up the beach.

I used to get the bus all the time with Dadu, just for the fun of it. Top deck, obviously. Sometimes we'd arrive somewhere and then turn straight round and get the bus back. *He* would be up for this adventure, not looking for reasons to squash it. Dadu would *love* the idea of day-tripping with an octopus in tow. And Ian would love it too.

Hassan jogged up to overtake me and turned around.

'A ferry is *very* different to a bus. It crosses a border! And you have no idea where to go after that!'

*Ugh. South!*

'Perhaps he *would* be fine in this sea, after all. That seems less of a risk than you on some international adventure!' He took in my sulky look and smiled.

'Look . . . come to mine for half an hour. My uncle used to keep fish. He had this huge tropical fish tank down the whole of his sitting room wall, and another one for freshwater fish in the dining room—'

I stopped walking. 'You've never told me that.'

'Er . . . no. Anyway, he was obsessed and had, like, a thousand books on fish-keeping and wild sea creatures and stuff, and he gave them all to me when he got rid of the tanks—'

'Why did he get rid of the tanks?' We were walking again, but I was totally intrigued by Hassan's secret fishy history.

'I dunno! I think my aunty didn't like them, or they took too much cleaning or something. *Anyway,* we can—'

'Why did he give *you* the books?'

'*Because,* I was really into his fish when I was little, OK? They were really cool, and I liked them a lot. So he thought I'd like the books. Which I did.'

'But you'd never been to the aquarium?'

'But I'd never been to the aquarium.' Hassan repeated and rolled his eyes at me in a mock patient way. I still thought it was pretty surprising if he was that into fish, though. No wonder he was so wide-eyed on that first visit.

'Is that why you're doing Project Free Ian with me?'

'Not really, no. You said you wanted help with something. And I wanted a break from talking about football for ten minutes, remember? But I do like hanging out with the fish, and I want to help Ian too, so that's a bonus, I guess. *Anyway,* are you gonna let me say what I want to say, or what? Cause I'm getting pretty cold now?'

We'd reached the top of our beach where we'd both dumped our bikes in a heap.

'OK, OK,' I dragged mine to the pavement and straddled it ready to set off, putting on my helmet as I listened.

'Just come to mine, look at the books. They have details of the water temperature required for each fish and stuff. We can find out the temp here and whether Ian would be OK. If he'd be fine, you've got to promise you'll drop this crazy France plan though, OK? If not, well . . . maybe we can research the route or something.' He shrugged, and I grinned.

'I just need to text Mum.'

Check out Hassan! So much for Darcie being the brainbox. *Water temperatures.* Although, I was secretly hoping the France plan was go – I wanted my epic octopus adventure to go international!

***

At Hassan's house, I'd taken charge of habitat, while he reluctantly looked at transport.

So far, my half-hearted search had revealed:

- Saltwater.
- Prefer coral reefs
- Ideal temperature range of 15 to 16°C.

My heart had skipped when I read they live in every ocean in the world. But the English Channel was *not* an ocean. Plus, I'm pretty sure it didn't have coral reefs. I thought again about those icy-looking waves crashing. It was November. It was cold. I closed the tab quickly before it ruined my France adventure.

Just to check, I looked up sea temperatures. November temperatures round here went down to 12.7 degrees. We couldn't risk it, and I wasn't going to argue about it, so I just didn't write that bit down.

'What have *you* got?' I leaned over Hassan's pad, covered with his tiny, scribbly hand writing.

'The ferry's a bad plan,' he said.

*Oh.*

I thought about that perfect white arrow, the sign that had showed me the way to France, that had started this whole new plan . . .

'You have to change, like, twenty times . . . and trek across Paris somehow for the train south. If you get the train to London and then the Eurotunnel, it's the same station. You should do that.'

I nodded, trying not to look nervous.

'It's still going to take more than twelve hours, Sash.'

He looked at me, but I stared back calmly. 'It's fine.'

'And we haven't even talked about how you'd move Ian!'

'It's *fine.*'

Hassan sighed. We were sitting at his glass dining table with a laptop, a tablet and a sprawling mass of fish books spread around us. And huge piles of snacks.

As soon as we'd walked through the door his Mum had leapt on me with hugs, as if she'd not seen me for years.

'You two look like you're going to die of cold!

Look at your cheeks! Give me your hands.' She'd grabbed my hands and scrubbed them between hers until the feeling had returned. Then stroked my cheek, whipped off my coat and ushered me to the table. She was a whirlwind of caring. By the time Hassan had found the books, she'd emptied about three packets of Doritos into bowls for us. Then she was dolloping yogurt into more bowls and dusting it with paprika.

'Mum, we're fine. Sashi's going home for dinner in a minute – we're just looking something up.'

'What are you talking about? You always come home from school starving! And where have you been anyway? Sashi's fingers nearly fell off in mine just then.'

I giggled. 'To the beach.'

'Sash, it's fine,' whispered Hassan. As if I minded chatting to his mum!

'In the *dark*?' she went on. 'Why ever would you—'

'Uh, Mum. *Science project.*'

'Oh! Of course. So many science projects! Well, let me get you some snacks.'

Hassan threw his arms wide and gestured

191

down at the snacks already on the table. Luckily, I knew full well he was a total mummy's boy at heart. And so did his mum.

'Thank you, that would be lovely!' I called out as she disappeared, and stuck my tongue out at Hassan.

We got on with our research, shovelling in Doritos by the handful.

If I was taking Ian on a day-long journey, I was going to need to feed him. Which meant we'd have to liberate *him* some snacks while we were at the aquarium.

**FACT: Octopuses are meat eaters. They eat pretty much anything, including crabs, crayfish, fish and even birds. There was a video on YouTube of an octopus wrestling a bald eagle!**

'Well, I'm not packing any birds for him to eat!' I said. 'Maybe we could take a bunch of sardines to keep him going?'

But Hassan was a "hard no" on that one. *Bit bossy.* He'd been hanging out with Darcie too much! He liked the idea of things you could put in your pocket – like hermit crabs. He'd been super keen on those little guys.

I presented my list of possible octopus-snacks and Hassan took it, his face full of doubt.

'I'm not sure this is a good idea.'

'What?'

'Just looking at it, it feels . . . wrong. Especially freeing the little guys just to feed them to Ian. Are we gonna peel the anemones off the rocks to take them? It sounds traumatic.'

'They don't have a happy life at the *aquarium*, being prodded by toddlers all day long!'

'Sashi, let's just take crab-sticks or something. From Co-Op. I'm sure it'll get him through one day.'

'*Fine.*' I was a little relieved. It would make everything much simpler. We were facing enough challenges already.

It was like Hassan read my mind, he twisted his mouth to the side. 'But, like . . . the journey too. There's no way you won't get caught. Or lost. You can't exactly just put him in your rucksack! Have you thought . . . maybe Darcie's right, Sash. Do you really want to do this? You've got so much going on at home, with your Dadu and everything. Maybe it's time to let this project rest . . .'

Tears sprang into my eyes before I could even think about trying to stop them, then I was so embarrassed it only made me cry more. *Then* I was so angry with myself for crying in embarrassment, *that* made the crying even worse.

I swiped at my face with a clenched fist.

'Have you been talking to Darcie, then? You sound just like her!'

He ducked his head and folded the list. 'She's worried about you, you know? And she misses you.'

The tears streamed faster, and I sank my face into my hands.

'Oh, Sashi, I'm sorry. Stop, please. I didn't mean to upset you.'

'Shut up! It's fine. I'm ANGRY!'

'With me?'

He couldn't look more injured. *Ugh!*

'Yes, with you! And with me, and with Darcie. I . . . don't want another half-finished project, OK? Like all my dad's abandoned schemes discarded round the house making my mum mad, like every homework project Darcie finishes for me. This was my *thing,* I wanted to really do this, to finish it, to get Ian home.

We can't let him down, he needs us! It's not a science project to him, OK? It's his future, a family, his whole *life*.'

'OK,' he held his hands up. 'I was just asking the question.'

The rage left me as quickly as it had bubbled up. I sighed. *Get it together, Sashi.* 'One more thing,' I sniffed hard. 'I think we just need to get on and do it now.' My voice shook. I didn't dare remind Hassan that Ian was being poisoned, I wasn't sure if he still believed that. 'This Sunday night. I'll set off first thing on Monday.'

'This Sunday? Are you serious?'

'We'll have all day Saturday and Sunday to get supplies. I have some pocket money saved, so you don't have to worry about that. Then we do it. Sunday night. Or I am anyway, with you or without you. You in?'

I put my hand in between us like Hassan had on the beach that first morning. He stared at my hand then shrugged, with that lopsided smile of his.

'I guess so,' he said, and placed his hand on mine. 'One, two, three, *Free Ian*!'

We both threw our hands in the air and I had to

bite my lip to stop more tears from erupting. It was becoming a bit of a habit. I was just wondering what on earth to say next, when Hassan's mum came bustling back into the room.

'What *are* you two shouting in here? Sashi, you'd better be making a move if your Mum's expecting you for dinner, although you're more than welcome to stay here, of course, we have plenty. Do you want me to ring her?'

'Oh no, I'm fine, thank you very much. You're right, I'd better be going.'

'Here you go, take a bottle or water for the journey, and a bag of crisps,' and she produced more snacks from somewhere and pressed them into my hands as I made for the door. I looked over my shoulder as I was bundled out, to check Hassan didn't have his fingers crossed or anything, but he winked at me calmly.

The plan was on. Four days to go. Me and Ian were off to France.

## CHAPTER 19

'You'll have to run this whole thing by me again, Sashimi-mine. It makes about as much sense as all this time you spend with those boring friends of yours instead of your darling dad.'

'*Daad*. I've had a homework project, I've been busy. And I'm twelve. I can't just sit around on the sofa all day doing puzzles with you.'

'Leave her alone, Manu. You were the one who said she should be allowed out more, you can't complain now she's gone and done it.'

'I know, I know, but I've missed her! She's my baby!'

Dad tried to grab me and smother me in a hug. I ducked away just in time and ran to the other side of the table, swatting the air as though a hug would be the world's most hideous experience. Which it would.

'Ah, she only wants me for my car. We've finally

reached that stage, Helen. When "parent" turns to "chauffeur". We knew it would happen."

'Don't be so dramatic.' Mum closed the book she was trying to read with a sigh, and pulled her feet up to tuck them under her on the chair. 'I thought we'd be chauffeuring somewhere slightly more exciting than the garden centre though, it has to be said.'

'That's what I said!' Dad chimed in. 'It makes no sense! Why do you want to spend your Saturday looking at tools and things?'

'Is this still the octopus thing, my love?' Mum's hands rested on the book in her lap. 'That's been going on for a while now, hasn't it? Is it for a science fair or something? It seems very involved.'

My cheeks burned, I wished she'd just start reading again – I was pretty sure Mum could sense my lies from a mile away. With Dad it was fine.

'It's a whole term thing,' I muttered. 'Don't worry about it.'

'Well, when do we get to see the finished thing?' She looked all excited.

'It's not going on display or anything . . .'

'But you need *fish tanks*?'

*Oh man, I need to seriously backtrack.*

'It's just one of the ideas Darcie had, to present our project. To class. Like a gimmick. We might not use it, we're still not 100% decided.'

Especially as carrying a fish task was going to be a complete nightmare. Would it go inside my wheelie suitcase? I couldn't imagine they would seal completely shut. We were hoping for inspiration to strike at the shop really.

'It's a bit of an expensive gimmick, darling, if you're not even going to use it.'

'It's OK, it's OK . . . we've all clubbed together, and we won't buy them if they're too much. And if we do buy one, we'll definitely use it, OK? And y'know, maybe I could have a fish and use the tank afterwards?'

'Oh!' Mum suddenly sat up straight. 'Well, that's a bit different. The tank would need cleaning, and you'd have to feed it, and—'

'I get how to look after a goldfish, Mum.'

'Yes, well. Don't do anything on a whim, OK? This house isn't the aquarium after all.' She settled back down and picked up her book again.

I breathed out. Maybe I was going to get away

with this. I turned to Dad. 'So, will you take us?'

'Sure thing, Little Fish. How could I resist a day out shopping with you and my favourite handsome nearly-nephew? Even if it is for fish tanks. Let's go get him, shall we?'

He shook his jeans pocket to make his car keys jangle and I ran to the door to get my coat.

***

I coasted down the aisle of the DIY shop like an ice skater. I loved wheeling on a trolley. Was there an age limit on that? Surely not. I bet even Dad would be doing it if no one was looking. I bet if you came here when it was about to close there would be some old person at the back of each aisle, skimming over the glossy tiles whistling a "wheeee" between their teeth.

I looked back at Dad now, walking in a fake casual way five steps behind us, swinging his arms and looking anywhere but at us. I rolled my eyes. He started rummaging around in the hosepipe fixings. As if he was about to start gardening – ha! We didn't even have a garden, just a paved square of courtyard with a few unloved pots in.

'Hassan,' I hissed. I launched the trolley forward, like a scooter, to catch him up. He shoved his phone in his pocket.

'So,' I said, 'we're going to need a tank that seals *completely* shut . . . no leaks. And a wheelbarrow . . .'

He span round, eyes wide. '*Wheelbarrow?*' He was whispering so quietly I could barely hear him. 'You're going to travel to the south of France with a *wheelbarrow*, Sash? Be serious.'

I rolled my eyes. 'Don't be ridiculous. Just to get him to my house, then we can pack up the tank in my suitcase with . . . er . . . socks and towels and things at home.'

'OK, I guess that makes sense. I don't think we're going to find a tank that doesn't leak, though. We should have planned this better.'

'Fine. Maybe he can go in a bin bag or something. Tied up really tight.'

'Oh man, there are so many ways this could go wrong. An octopus-filled water balloon in a wheelbarrow! And on the train? Are we just going to balance the bin bag on top of your suitcase and wobble out with it . . .? What if it rolls off?'

*Eeesh.* 'Good point. Maybe we need rope? Or bungee cords! With bungees we could strap it down nice and tight.'

'Right. Bungee cord. Gottya.'

Hassan's walk was just like Dad's. All unhurried and casual, despite the frantic conversation. With a lurch of embarrassment it struck me it was *Hassan* my dad was copying with his lopey stride. *Everyone* wanted a piece of Hassan's "cool". *Mortifying.*

But Hassan had stopped walking now. He squeaked the toe of his trainer on the shiny floor.

'This is a bad idea, Sashi, sorry. Bin bags and bungee cord? It's a mess.'

'Well, how else are we gonna do it?'

'Let's just look and see what we can find. Maybe they have some kind of octo-travel case in here somewhere!' He laughed at himself.

*Phew.* I needed him on side.

'If we *really* can't find anything else we can think about your tottering tower of octopus bags!' He gave me a cheesy thumbs up, and I breathed a sigh of relief. *Still on.*

'And we're really doing this tomorrow?' he asked.

'YES!' I was jumping with excitement.

Hassan got out his phone again and started texting furiously.

'Someone special?' I teased.

He actually went a bit pink; maybe he felt guilty for interrupting our trip. 'Er, no . . . just . . . some of the football lads. I had to miss training, so, well, they're giving me grief.'

I could imagine the abuse Luka would dish out for him skipping football to go shopping with a girl. But Hassan was here anyway. He'd even been hanging out with me at school a bit since he stood up to Luka under the oak tree. I'd thought Hassan was intimidated by no one. I'd been wrong then, but it looked like I was right now.

'Ah, well, send them my love!' I laughed, ramming him with my shoulder. 'Where shall we start?' I scanned the overhead signs. '"Kitchens and Bathrooms"?'

'No way. That's DIY stuff to *build* kitchens and bathrooms. I thought we were going to the garden bit? Or we could try the "Storage" section? That sounds hopeful?'

*Buzz buzz.*

Now it was my phone's turn to interrupt us. I slipped it from my pocket. *Darcie*. My heart jumped to my throat. I'd managed to avoid her all week at school, which hadn't been easy.

'Hang on a sec,' I said to Hassan, and jumped both feet up on the trolley to coast to an empty corner of the shop. I didn't trust my emotions and certainly didn't want them on display to Hassan.

Swipe.

**DARCIE:** Hey there Sash-mash, missed you this week, how's it going? Hassan says PFI is still on?

Huh. Does he?

**ME:** When have you spoken to Hassan?

**DARCIE:** I see him at school jelly-brains! And we text sometimes.

That was a strange thought. They'd never "seen each other at school" before. I guess it was nice they were friends now.

**DARCIE:** You can still run stuff by me if you like. I'm still your friend even if I'm not doing the project. When are we going to hang?

**ME:** Look, Darcie, we're busy right now, OK? Maybe we can talk later.

**DARCIE**: OK, well, sounds like you've got it covered anyway, wheelbarrows and whatever, just the offer's there if you want to run the plan by me OK? Just saying.

*Ugh!* Why does she make everything sound so stupid? "Wheelbarrows and whatever". It was going to work!

**ME**: Look, you wanted out, so just butt out. I don't need your advice, OK? I've got this.

I clicked my phone off before I saw any more responses. I didn't need Darcie putting a downer on everything. She didn't even know Phase Two of the plan: fast-tracking Ian straight to the Med, how awesome it was going to be.

'Sashi, c'mere!' Hassan slid sideways about three metres in a perfectly elegant glide down the aisle ending exactly in front of the trolley. 'I think I've found the perfect thing.'

'Perfect how?'

'Come see. It's a watertight storage trunk on wheels! And it's blacked out. Ian will feel safe, and no one will be able to see what we're doing.' He was bouncing. 'We fill it up, seal it shut, wheel it out.

No balancing, no strapping, no packing up with socks . . . You can get on the train with it, and wheel it into the sea at the other end. Ian can swim straight out. What do you think?'

I'd never heard Hassan so hyped! He was right though, it was perfect.

I turned round to see where Dad was – he'd made himself at home, spread out on one of the display-only sunloungers. Now I just had to explain to him why we'd come in for a fish tank and were leaving with a 50-litre storage trunk on wheels.

# CHAPTER 20

It was tonight. Actually tonight. As in – I took out my phone to check the time – 12:30 p.m. – then counted on my fingers. Six and a half hours to go! Me and Hassan had arranged to meet at 7 p.m. We reckoned the seafront would be quietest after all the families had gone home, but before the grown-ups came out.

So soon! I span in a circle on our front path, then looked at my phone screen again before pressing it to my chest – *no. Resist the temptation.* I really wanted to call Darce so I could share this with her – it felt so wrong that she wasn't involved. But I had to resist. *Resist, resist, resist.* I could tell her all about it when I was back, when it was a done deal.

Me and Hassan had just been down the beach to half-fill his fancy storage container with seawater. Then we'd hidden it next to the bins behind the aquarium – Ian himself would be proud of our camouflaging skills.

The plan was to skim off some familiar water from his aquarium tank, to give him a chance to "acclimatise" on the journey, and top it up with seawater we'd collected. That was something from Hassan's many fish books. Apparently, fish need to get used to stuff gradually. Presumably the same was true with octopuses? I'd even put some shells in the bottom to make him feel at home.

**FACT: Octopus dens are often surrounded with empty shells and rocks as well as found objects like sea glass, plastics or bottles.**

We'd also hidden a rucksack with some gloves we'd picked up at the garden centre – heavy duty, waterproof gloves that came up to our elbows – a retractable net and one of my dad's smaller toolkits, with wrenches and stuff. Just in case. Hassan was at home now, spending all his savings to buy my Eurostar and train tickets. After he decided he couldn't make the trip with me he'd said it was the least he could do. Besides, I knew well enough that my mum *always* checked my internet search history.

Now I just had to kill time. Six and half hours of time! I was going to explode.

I let myself into the house and could hear the ringing peal of Mum's laughter. There were two matching blond blurs through the marbled glass of the living room door instead of just Mum's one. I felt a pang of jealousy.

*Was it?*

I paused with my fingers on the glass, an uneasy feeling sloshing in my stomach. The low rumble of Dad's voice, then an unmistakeable high-pitched singsong.

*It was.*

I pushed open the door, and all three of them turned to look at me – their smiles frozen.

I opened my mouth but felt like I might be sick, so closed it again.

'Sashi, Darcie popped round to see you,' Mum stood up. 'Do you girls want some snacks? You can eat them here? Take them up ...?'

'Up?' I was glued to the spot. *Why was she here? So much for not talking to her until it was a done deal!*

'C'mon, let's go to your room and hang for a bit.'

Darcie leapt up and grabbed me on her way through the door, nearly knocking me over.

'Why?'

*'Why?'* She gave me a look. This one meant: "let's not do this in front of your parents, we can talk about it upstairs".

She had a point.

'Fine.'

'We're OK for snacks, thanks,' Darcie called over her shoulder as she pulled me up the stairs.

Maybe we could not talk about tonight's plan at all. Just gossip about school, instead? We could plan our future careers and what our houses would be like and our style assessments of each kid in our year. The usual. There need be no mention of Ian or Eurostar or aquariums at all. With each step up the stairs I hoped that was true. I watched the confident way she bounced as she walked, her hair swinging behind her, the secret-filled look she gave me over her shoulder – I missed my friend. I missed *having* a best friend. Had it really been less than a week?

She slumped down cross-legged on my bed like she had a trillion times before.

'So, tell me the plan.'

I shoved all the clothes off my wheeled desk chair and sat down on that. 'Let's not talk about it. What have *you* been up to?'

'Seriously, Sash-mash, I want to know. When's the big release?' She was fiddling with her hair, sorting through the ends looking for splits, rather than looking at me.

I got up and bounced down next to her instead.

'Hassan's such a doofus, he won't do anything even vaguely adventurous. I think he needs you there to show-off in front of.' I elbowed her in the ribs, and she finally dropped her hair and side-eyed me.

'How much more adventurous do you want him to *be*? You already have him breaking and entering for you! Do want him to abseil in in a tutu?'

I giggled. *'That's* a vision I need to shake. But yeah, y'know . . . just a small helicopter hijack, parachute in, it's not too much to ask, right?' I grinned and flopped back on my bed, tension melting away. 'It's so weird that you and him are friends now,' I mused. 'When are you going to start sitting with the football team at lunch?'

'You are so full of rubbish, Sash-a-lac. Literally, the only thing we have in common is that we're both Team Sashi. All we ever talk about is you.'

I threw my hands up. *As IF.*

Darcie lay back too and rolled on her side to look at me. 'C'mon, though. I know I'm not involved any more, but you can still tell me when you're doing it.'

'Tonight! Tonight, OK? But let's not talk about it.'

Darcie sat back up. 'Sashi, please sit up.' Her voice had gone quiet, 'I want to talk to you.'

I rolled over on to my front and buried my face in the duvet. It was just going to be the same conversation we'd had in the juice bar. She put a hand on my back and rocked me from side to side.

'Sashi, please.'

'Ugggggggh,' I groaned. 'Do we have to do this?' I dragged myself up to sitting, but scooted back against the wall. 'I've already heard your many arguments.'

'Did you? I mean, did you actually *listen*?'

'Yes!'

'The aquarium isn't somewhere Ian needs to be rescued from. I've learnt so much from Martha.'

'Martha! *Please.*'

'Sashi, honestly – they do loads of work rescuing animals that need help, that have been injured by fishing gear, or are sick or stranded or whatever. Then they rehabilitate them and release them back into the wild themselves – they have a whole programme set up to do just that. Other species, they breed in captivity with the aim of releasing some of those into the wild too. They're on the same side as you. They do so much conservation work . . . the bit of the aquarium you see is just a tiny part of it.'

'I don't even know what you're *talking* about.' I covered my face. 'They re-what?'

'It doesn't matter – rehabilitate – they get them back on their feet, er, tentacles.' She threw me a sparkly look. '. . . make them better, whatever, but they release them when they're ready – if that's the best thing for them.'

'That sounds like advertising. Dad would say that's the kind of stuff they put on their website to make themselves sound all goody and right-on. Who knows if it's true or not?'

'Martha showed me a whole load of stuff; I trust her.'

'Yeah, well you and Martha make a great pair.'

'Argh! I never thought you'd actually go through with this! This is so all my fault.'

*What?*

Darcie rose up to kneeling on the bed and fixed me with a look. 'Sashi, I don't want you to get caught. You could get in so much trouble.'

'Don't pretend this is about me, now. You probably just don't want Martha to lose her job!'

'Oh, come *on*!' Darcie gripped a handful of duvet and threw it down again. 'If you could give me *one* good reason why you're doing this, then maybe I could back you . . . but you can't!'

I screwed my eyes shut. Darcie thought she had the answers to everything. All this stuff about their save-everyone work . . . maybe it was true. Maybe they *did* do some good stuff. But it wasn't the right thing for *Ian* – only I knew that. How could I explain that to her? I opened my eyes and glanced up at the wardrobe.

There was only one way to show her what I knew, and why I had to do it. I just had to hope she'd understand.

\*\*\*

214

I dragged the sketchbook down from my wardrobe shelf and took it out of the bags I kept it in.

'What's this? I don't get it.'

'Give me a sec, will you? I'll explain.'

I stroked the front cover. It was a gorgeous fabric book that Dadu had bought me for Christmas the year before last, in a mossy green. The sketchbook buying had become a tradition since that first one he'd drawn empty comic-book frames in. But this was the last one he'd given me . . . he'd already been too ill by last December.

I loved running my fingers over the texture of it, like tree bark. And now this book contained the most magical thing that had ever happened to me.

I was going to share it! At last! A spark of excitement lit inside me. It had been weird keeping it from Darcie – we usually told each other every detail of our lives, down to how disappointing that morning's Weetabix had been. We'd never had a secret from each other before. And such a huge one – no wonder everything had gone weird! I just wanted the two of us to be silly together again, for everything to go back to normal. Maybe when I showed her the book, it would?

Except . . . this was *Darcie STEM-warrior* we were talking about. The Darcie that laughed in the face of horoscopes and hated superstitious magpie rhymes. Not that what had happened with Ian was magic or anything, but there wasn't exactly proof either.

'Sashi, are you going to sit there staring at some mysterious book and ignoring me? Or are you going to tell me what on earth all this is about?' She was still angry.

'Right . . .'

'What can that book possibly have to do with your jailbreak-an-octopus plan?'

'Just listen, OK?'

And I told her about my first trip to the aquarium with Dad, about the strange feeling I'd had looking at Ian. About that feverish vision, and waking up, and what I'd found in my sketchbook in the morning. About the other time it'd happened too, and what Ian had been trying to tell me. About how unhappy he was, how the aquarium wasn't the right place for him and how he needed to get home.

I hadn't dared to look at her face as I'd been talking, instead I'd focused on her frantically

216

swinging red-socked foot. I risked looking up. Darcie was biting her lip, but for once in my life I really couldn't read the look she was giving me.

'Look,' I said, holding the book out to her, then crossing the room to sit back on the desk chair. Giving her some space.

Darcie took the book and turned the pages slowly, studying each picture then studying them again.

'Look,' I said, reaching over to turn the pages back to the start. 'I drew those things that look like bunches of grapes. I googled it afterwards, and that's what octopus *eggs* look like – can you believe it? I had no idea. I had no way of knowing that . . . which is how I know for sure that Ian *communicated* the images to me.'

She flipped a page again to the one showing keeper-creep and the poison, and I'm sure her face hardened a little.

I couldn't lose her. I needed to speak Darcie-language . . .

'My dad said plenty of people in the past thought octopuses were psychic, right? There's still so much we don't know about their brains. They're on a completely different *evolutionary path* to us, did you know that? So it's quite pos—'

'I know that,' she interrupted. *Well, of course she did.* Still.

Darcie looked pale. Was she feeling guilty? I wished she would say something.

Instead, she took the pages in her long fingers and, in a sudden movement, ripped right down the middle of my drawings.

I jumped up, gasping and knocking the chair over behind me. I tried to grab the book, but Darcie jumped on to the bed.

'No!' she cried, and ripped again and again, white peels of paper falling to the bed and the floor around her. Her teeth were bared and tears wet her face.

'What . . .? Why . . .? Just *stop!*' I sank down to the carpet, picking up slivers of pictures. 'Darcie, no! Please.' She kept ripping and ripping. Magical messages reduced to curls of litter.

Then a bubble of rage surged up in me and I jumped back up. 'You evil *cow!*' I started hitting at her legs and anything I could reach as she backed away from me, throwing the book over my head on to the floor behind me.

'It's all a *lie*, Sashi.' She tried to grab my hands, but I wasn't going to let her have them. 'I can't let you do this based on *that*.'

She spat the "that" as though the book were evil. As though Ian had been blackmailing me or something.

She jumped down from the bed, so we were eye to eye, still trying to grab my hands as I thrashed at her. 'This is all about your Dadu, you know?'

*'What?'*

I was so shocked I stopped struggling long enough for her to grab me. She pulled me down to sit on the bed, still pinning my hands. I tried to squirm away, but she was bigger than me.

She took a breath and made this huge patronising effort to use a calm voice. 'Freeing Ian isn't going to set your Dadu free, Sash-a-lac, and there's no magic way to communicate with either of them.'

'Argh!!!' I managed to wrench myself free from her grip and shake her off me.

I didn't have to sit here and listen to this. What was she talking about? This had nothing to do with Dadu.

If Dadu was psychic I would never leave the home he was in. But he wasn't, *Ian* was. Ugh! Everything was so confusing.

'You're in denial. I'm sorry, but someone had to say something.'

'Get out, OK? I don't want you to come here. Ever again.'

'And it's all my fault, pushing you into a stupid distraction . . .'

'Darcie—'

'Sashi, listen – one more thing, please.'

'Get *out!*'

'OK! I'm going. But . . . life sciences.'

'*What?*'

She spoke fast. 'Don't you remember that video we watched in life sciences, and you doodled all the way through and looked out the window?'

'Well, probably not then, brainbox – it doesn't sound like I was exactly into it. Didn't I just ask you to *go*?'

'Sashi, it showed us scenes of octopus caves with eggs just like that – like bunches of grapes. You watched it; I was there. At the end of last year. You even sketched some in your margin.'

'Get *out!*' I screamed so loud I heard a door open and shut downstairs, but I didn't care.

I slammed my own bedroom door so close and hard behind Darcie as she left, I'm surprised I didn't trap her finger.

It bounced back open again and I threw myself down on my bed in a pile of the ripped paper and cried.

# CHAPTER 21

The minute I heard the front door close behind Darcie, I dragged myself off my bed. I knew where I needed to go. I charged down the stairs, blocking out concerned calls from Mum and Dad. They'd clearly jumped to their feet as soon as they heard me coming, but I didn't have time for that. I just had to ignore them as I chased out of the house after her. *No time, no time.* But while Darcie would have turned left to go to her house, I grabbed my bike and turned right.

I needed proof. I needed me to be right and her to be wrong. *Denial! As IF.*

*But, but but . . .*

Thoughts of the video we'd watched at school crackled through my body like electricity. I did remember watching it, and I could vaguely see the underwater scenes. What else? Ohhhh, if it did have eggs in, that changed everything.

How long had I used that as absolute proof?

Every time a doubt had edged to the corner of my brain, I'd squashed it flat with that picture in my sketchbook – those eggs I couldn't possibly have known about without Ian's help. But now Darcie had opened new possibilities that maybe I *had* known . . .

*Argh!* I needed to get rid of all these doubts she'd put in my brain; the tentacles of uncertainty that were weaving through my thoughts, overturning weeks of planning. I needed Ian. And he absolutely had to talk to me. *Please, please.* It was the least he could do.

It wasn't long before I was back at the aquarium, back in my familiar spot, pressed up against Ian's tank, eyes locked with my octopus friend.

*'Talk to me.'*

I whispered it at him. Thought it at him, shouting in my mind. Begged him.

I closed my eyes. How did it normally happen? There was a prickle, a cold sweat, an undeniable *feeling.* And I just knew.

I needed that feeling now. 'C'mon, Ian, please. Help me.' I hissed it through my teeth, ignoring the people pooling around me, waiting for their turn.

But nothing.

He was just an octopus, in a tank, floating around.

His eyes looked like black and white discs; flat buttons, sewn on to a stuffed toy, hiding nothing. Telling me nothing.

I could have smashed the glass with my bare fists.

It was like a bubble had popped; a switch had been flicked. Darcie had told me about that life sciences video and now everything was different.

I still wasn't ready to give up entirely. I stayed, willing and waiting for that sensation to pass over me. *Maybe he just wasn't ready.* I told myself that, but somehow I knew differently. I watched him as he spun gracefully across the tank. I stood back as people came and went, pointing and squealing at him. I tried to keep eye contact, wherever I stood, gazing into his bulbous eyes. I watched as he retreated to the back of his tank, curled up inside his wheel, rose back out again.

*Please, Ian.*

Nothing.

I checked my phone – I'd been there for an hour. No prickles. No sweat. No feelings. How long should I wait? That's when I caught sight of Martha approaching – I did *not* want to talk to *her*. With one last look at Ian, I left.

*** 

Back home, back on my bed, I clutched the moss green sketchbook, with my pencil in my hand, hoping some message had got through without me realising. Maybe I'd got used to the feeling and didn't even notice it any more? He just beamed those messages straight in there, like oxygen. *Right?*

My hand shook as I held it to one of the blank pages left un-ripped. I waited. What had happened before? Had it moved by itself? Surely not. I couldn't really remember. I'd just known what to draw. Well, I had to know now . . . I *had* to.

I started to sketch out Ian's beautiful twisting form but it looked all wrong and I scrubbed it out. I should start with his eyes – before today I thought I knew those best, but there was no message to tell. I drew tanks and then drew myself smashing them, dead fish on the floor. I scrubbed those out too. My stomach clenched tight as my pencil formed a curl of hair – keeper creep . . .

Michael – had I been wrong about that too? I drew torn pieces of sketchbook paper catching the air and spiralling out the window and off to sea.

I had to accept it. My brain wasn't full of magical pictures; it was full of questions. The eggs . . . the video . . . how could I possibly believe this was all real if that was true?

My workbooks from last year were still in an un-sorted pile under my bed. I dropped heavily to the floor and dragged them out. The life sciences book was a dull, dusty red – flicking through it I already knew what I'd find. Every page was dark with illustrations. Leaves, trees, minibeasts, seahorses, fish, octopuses – octopus eggs. Like grapes. Strung up in a cave.

I shut the book and pushed it back under my bed. So, there you go, that question was answered. Now others flooded my brain, all stirred up by Darcie. Did the aquarium really release animals into the wild when they were ready? Why hadn't they released Ian? Was he really happy there? And what did *any* of this have to do with Dadu?

The thought of Dadu hollowed a space in my stomach that ached with a longing to see him. It had been five weeks. I'd marked them on a calendar by my bed. I couldn't bear to think how much worse he might have got in five weeks. Had Mum still been secretly visiting him? We hadn't talked about it since my duvet day. I should ask her.

I crept down the stairs, much more quietly this time. If Mum and Dad were in separate rooms, I didn't want Dad to hear me so I could talk to Mum alone. But there was a soft rumble of conversation from the living room and the shushing sound of my name caught my attention. I sat down on the stairs and strained to listen.

'We should take her to see him again, Manu, she's clearly still so upset by it. We shouldn't have stopped the visits so suddenly.'

Were they talking about *Dadu*? What were the chances? Psychics everywhere. I should go in, tell them "yes" . . .

'No. *No*, Helen, we're not going to do that . . . Sorry!' By the way Dad raised his voice on the last word I could tell Mum had opened her mouth to object, I could virtually see his raised hands.

'He's *my* father and I decide this one. It's final. It's just . . .'

Dad carried on laying down the law, but I didn't

want to hear it. I turned and scurried back upstairs.

Why had I not been asking them about this every day for the past five weeks? I should have been fighting to see him, putting all my energy into that instead of this ridiculous octopus project. Oh *man*! Distraction. All Darcie's rubbish about needing a distraction! In fact, distraction was the last thing I needed. I should have been facing the truth! Focusing on Dadu. This was all her fault!

Despite everything, all I really wanted was to talk to Darcie about it. But I also never wanted to see her again, so that was going to be tricky.

Maybe I could just text? I picked up my phone – not to actually do it, just to think about it – but saw the time. 5:41.

*5:41*

Project Free Ian was supposed to be happening in . . . I screwed up my face and flexed my mental fingers . . . nineteen, er, *oh no*, one hour and nineteen minutes.

Hassan would be finishing his tea, then putting on his black zip-up hoodie, ready to go stealth-mode. What were we doing? We had to call it off.

But how could I tell Hassan that, after everything?

What would he think of me? Or all the time he'd spent on this?

A wave of nausea hit me. *The money for the tickets!*

I cautiously unlocked my phone screen and stared down at it. How was I even going to put this? I couldn't. We'd have to talk.

**ME:** Hassan. Call me as soon as you get this, thx

I sat down with my phone in my lap. I was sweating. He didn't call.

5:50.

**ME:** If you've not bought the tickets yet — DON'T!

6:00.

**ME:** Urgent — Change of plan. Call me.

6:15.

**ME:** Hassan . . .!!! Where are you???? Have you lost your phone??

6:30.

I'd been to the loo about ten times now and my heart was fluttering like it was full of moths. This was Not Good. Five more minutes and I'd have to go. *C'mon, c'mon, c'mon Hassan – call me!*

What if he gets there without me and gets started? I leapt to my feet and dragged on the clothes.

I'd set aside for the night. Black jeans, black t-shirt, black hoodie, black snood to cover my face. Like a proper crim. Which is what we'd be if we went through with this. Ohhhhhhhhhh . . . why was that only obvious to me now?

I needed to get to the aquarium first and make sure my friend didn't get in trouble. All because of me.

# PART
# THREE

# CHAPTER 22

Right now, I only knew one thing clearly: I had to stop Hassan before it was too late.

I'd never ridden so fast, but it wasn't fast enough.

**FACT: The giant Pacific octopus can reach speeds of 40 kmph.**

*I* could do with some jet-propulsion round about now.

With every turn of my pedals, a different image filled my brain.

*Hassan in his hoodie, being stopped by police.*

I skidded my bike round a corner too fast and the back wheel nearly flew out behind me. It'd started to drizzle, and the roads were glistening with damp in the glow from the streetlights.

*Hassan's face freeze-framed in a CCTV image and printed out in the local newspaper.*

I hammered the brakes at a red light I'd nearly

missed and put my foot to the floor, my knee bouncing with impatience.

*Hassan smashing a tank with a wrench from my dad's toolkit. Water flooding out on to the floor of the aquarium.*

I edged forwards. *C'mon light, turn green.* The light changed and I pushed away, standing on the pedals to accelerate harder. I was on the coast road now and getting closer to our meeting point.

*Hassan wrestling Ian into the black storage trunk, suckered arms circling his.*

There were plenty of cars about, but the pavements were quiet. There were normally tons of pedestrians walking up and down here, so we'd been right with our choice of time. What time was it now? Why didn't I have a watch? I couldn't exactly get my phone out while I was cycling. Was it past seven yet? Surely Hassan wouldn't start without me . . . he would wait – right?

*Hassan just testing out the door code, being forced to the ground by security.*

I wanted to close my eyes to block the images out, but I had to keep looking at the road – my cycling was shaky enough already. Instead I gritted my teeth – the images weren't real. None of this was happening. I'd left early. I would be there first. And he would wait. The plan was to meet on the beach. If he was there already, he'd be on the beach. *But, but, but* . . .

A nugget of doubt had lodged in my brain. Hassan *did* like to be the knight in shining armour. There was a small chance, just a chance, he could try and step in, so I didn't have to – remove the risk from me. He might even have gone there early . . . maybe that's why his phone was off?

The minute *this* thought sailed through my brain, my insides did a double flip and I nearly fell off my bike with the sudden need to run to the nearest bathroom. *Hold it together, Sashi.* I stepped up my speed, I could see a red light ahead, but it was just a pedestrian crossing, so I mounted the pavement and skimmed round it. Mum would absolutely kill me, and I whispered a silent apology to her in my head. It had to be OK – I was trying to stop something much worse happening. But as I bounced back down, my front wheel landed in the gutter with an ominous popping sound and my bike started to shake.

A car thundered past me, covering me with spray as I ground to a halt, one foot on the pavement, and looked down. Flat tyre.

*Seriously? Now?* I growled my frustration into the dark sky, then hauled my useless bike on to the pavement and started pushing it. *Too slow.* I tried to run with it, but the pedals slammed repeatedly into my shins and the wheel was making a horrible sound. There were a couple of bikes chained to the railings that ran along the seafront. I bumped my bike over to them. *"Lock it",* said my dad's voice in my head, and I reluctantly unclipped the U-lock. I didn't know how long I was going to leave it here for, after all.

It wasn't too much further; I'd been nearly there. I tried to ignore the throb from my pedal-battered shins as I started running down the wet pavement. My chest burned with the effort. I pulled off my snood to gulp some cool air, and carried on running – hands flapping loose, feet slapping hard on the road. Then I saw the aquarium ahead and managed a spurt. Hassan should be just beyond it on the beach.

*Please be there, please be there, please be there. Please have waited.* I just needed him to be OK and not heading to jail because of me and my stupid, made-up project. How could I forgive myself if anything happened to him?

I stumbled breathless on to the beach. Someone was sitting on the stones. *Please be Hassan.* Not in black though, in a fancy wool coat. *Who is it?* Hair combed neatly into place. *Definitely Hassan.* But . . . was he going to walk in looking like that? What'd happened to "stealth mode"? I was bent double, raking in breaths as fast as I could, my lungs screaming for more air than I could get them. *As soon as I get my breath back, I'm going to tell him it's off.*

'Hassan,' I whispered. But even one word was too much, and I exploded in a lung-twisting fit of coughs.

He turned at his name and stood to walk towards me – he wasn't alone. Hassan smiled as he approached me . . . but standing up behind him was Darcie.

She spoke before he did, raising her hands as if to stop any protest before it began, even though I was coughing too much to even speak.

'I'm sorry, Sashi. I couldn't let you do this. I never thought it would go this far. I'm really sorry.'

\*\*\*

If I hadn't been choking already, I would have choked on that.

Still trying to breathe, I could only manage to shake my head, hands on my knees. Hassan bent over me and took me by the shoulders.

'Are you OK?'

I dragged in a massive breath, enough to lean past Hassan and spit out, 'What are you doing here?' at Darcie.

Her cheeks were pink. 'I just said, didn't I?' Her eyes were welling with tears. *For goodness' sake.*

I gripped Hassan back and checked him from head to toe – he was really here. Not in a police cell, not knocked out on the floor of the aquarium, not blustering in all keen. So much for a knight in shining armour! My relief was edged with a small twang of disappointment at that. Just a tiny one. He hadn't even shown up in black . . . he'd had no intention of doing it at all! He could at least have messaged and saved me the bike ride from hell.

'Didn't you get my texts?' I lifted my chin.

'You texted?' He started fumbling for his phone, then pulled it out and stared at the screen for a minute, thumb tapping away.

Now I'd stopped moving at maximum speed, cold seeped into every part of my body. The moon was nearly full and joined the streetlamps to light the beach like a stage, reflecting off the sea in broken chunks, but also off each glossy pebble around us. It gave our little scene an even more dramatic edge – especially with the over-the-top soundtrack of crashing waves and screeching seagulls. *As if this wasn't high drama enough!* I shivered.

'Where were you?' I asked. 'I thought maybe you'd gone in early.' My voice faltered. Looking at him in his fancy dad-coat, I was clearly an idiot for even thinking it.

'Yeah, I was with Darcie, sorry. I didn't hear—'

I pulled away from him, out of the grip of the hand that was still on me. I hadn't thought I could feel worse today.

'Were you ever going to do this? Is this all some

big joke to you both? Have you been laughing at me together this entire time?'

Darcie had sat back down on the beach, her blonde hair streaming over her bent knees. It must have been even colder down there.

'I don't even know what to say to you any more, Sashi,' she said. 'Just tell me you're not going in there, will you?'

'I don't need you here, Darcie! I had this handled.'

They both gawped at me, total disbelief written all over their faces.

'I've just run half the blinking coast road to tell Hassan the plan is off, OK?'

'Oh, is that the "change of plan"?' Hassan scrolled back through his messages.

'YES!' I needed to sit down too; my legs were jelly.

'Hey,' Hassan's voice was soft. 'I didn't get them.'

I had no idea what he was on about.

'The Eurostar tickets . . .' He held up his phone. 'You said, "*If you've not bought the tickets yet*". I . . . I didn't.'

I shook my head. *Details.*

I was starting to shiver violently, and my teeth were

chattering. But I couldn't, *wouldn't*, sit next to Darcie.

'Why can't you just butt out and leave me alone, Darcie? You don't have to run my life. I get it, OK? I made a stupid mistake and I'm here to fix it. But oh, no . . . you're here first, of course you are. Because you're even better at living my own life than I am!' I was getting into my stride, anger rising as I spoke. 'At fixing *my* mistakes, at saving my friends – you won't even let me do that myself! You have to control everything! If you're so much better at being me than *me*, why were you even friends with me in the first place?' *Why was she?*

A sound like a sob erupted from the blonde heap on the stones. *Really?*

'Hey, girls, now come on a minute.'

'Ugh! Don't "girls" us, Hassan! Give me a break!'

'Fine, whatever, but you need to talk. We should have talked about all this ages ago. Together.' He shot Darcie what could almost have been an angry look, if I didn't know better. 'Sashi, I asked Darcie to come, OK. I . . . I had some . . . er . . . *concerns*. And we've been working together on—'

'*What?*'

Darcie lifted her head. 'Oh, *don't*. Hassan, I don't think now's the moment. We said we weren't going to say anything . . .'

'Yeah, but I think it's obvious keeping her in the dark wasn't the best plan, was it? She's freaking out!'

'TOO RIGHT I'M FREAKING OUT!'

'Wait, we've just been meeting up to talk it over and—'

'TALK IT OVER?'

This was getting worse by the second. I span around on the spot. Should I just walk away? This was a joke . . . a total joke.

Or *I* was.

'Yeah, so hilarious! The mad octopus girl—'

'Sashi, no!' Darcie was on her feet and stepping towards me, long fingers reaching out. She was definitely crying.

I was *not* going to cry; I wouldn't give her that. I refused.

'Sashi, you're my best friend. Why would I laugh at you? I was worried about you.'

'Oh c'mon! *Best friends*, don't rip up each other's most precious possessions. *Best friends*, don't

talk about each other behind their backs, sharing
*"concerns"* – why didn't you just talk to *me*?'

'I tried! You wouldn't listen!' She groaned.
'I'm so sorry. I thought the plan would fizzle out
by itself, but you seemed to get more and more
determined . . . I . . . I didn't know what to do. I was
really worried you'd get arrested or something.
And now, France!'

The shakes were getting worse, my whole body
was vibrating like a road drill. I rubbed my arms.

Hassan took another step towards me. 'I *wanted* to
be there too, Sash. I've had fun. It wasn't like all that.'
He reached out as though he was going to try and
hug me again, but I raised my hands and pushed him
away from me, hard, turning back to Darcie.

'So what was your grand plan tonight, anyway?
Turn up and ask me nicely? If I'd wanted to do this,
I didn't need Hassan – I don't need either of you!
How were you planning to stop me?'

Gravel crunched behind me, and I turned.

'Are we all OK here? It looks like it might be getting
a little heated?'

*Mum and Dad. How . . .? What . . .?*

I stared into my dad's concerned face, then turned to Darcie to catch a fleeting look of panic between her and Hassan.

So, that's how they were going to stop me.

Heat filled my body faster than a forest fire — all the night's cold and shakes chased out in one second flat, leaving my fingers tingling and my eyes burning.

'You—'

'Sashi, sunshine, you need to calm down and come walk with me for a minute.' My dad took hold of my hand like he used to, and mine felt tiny, still, in his dry, warm one. 'Your friends have done you a big favour and I think in a minute we're all going to get some food, but first you're going to walk a bit with me.'

'They are NOT my friends.'

'Walk with me.' He looked super stern. *Oh no — did he know why I was here?* I flashed a quick look at Darcie and her face confirmed it. The bottom of my stomach fell out.

'Dad, I can explain the whole thing. I came here to—'

'It doesn't matter, it's all over now. It's all over.'

He was using the voice he would use if I were sick, and was dragging me by the hand up the beach, away from the others. I swung around to look over my shoulder and saw Mum with Hassan and Darcie. She put her arm around Darcie's shoulders and pulled her into a hug, while I was being dragged away.

What *was* this? Was I being taken off for punishment?

'Dad, what's Mum—'

'Just walk with me, Sashi. It's all over now.'

# CHAPTER 23

'Dad, I don't *want* to walk with you.' I tried to pull my hand out of his but he held me firm, still tugging me forwards. 'I need to go back!'

Dad paused for a beat. 'To apologise?'

'No way! To tell her what I think of . . . of . . .' I gestured at Dad. Him and Mum being here. Darcie having involved them. '. . . all this!'

Dad pursed his lips and pushed on. 'Exactly, Sashi. That's why we're walking.'

'*Daaaad,*' I was yelling and stamping.

Dad stopped and turned to face me, annoyingly calm.

'You nearly did a very, very stupid thing, Sashi. And dangerous. Don't think we're not going to be talking about that later. But, for now, I need you to take a few deep breaths and then we can go and sit down and talk. Darcie—'

'Dad, I wasn't going to—'

'Stop! I don't want to hear excuses! Darcie is a very good friend to you—'

'How can you say that wh—'

'*Sashi.*' His eyes looked fiercer than I'd ever seen, and my words evaporated in my mouth. I shrank away from this new, serious Dad. He was like he'd been when he made that decision about Dadu, in the car, and wouldn't hear arguments. My normal, playful Dad was a million miles away.

'This is not a time for you to be interrupting me, do you understand? Try *listening* to what I'm saying to you and accepting the truth. I repeat: Darcie is a very good friend to you. She brought us here because she was scared for you. *And* she persuaded me I shouldn't be angry.' *You'd be less angry if she hadn't TOLD you!* 'At least until she's said whatever it is she wants to say!'

Despite his denials about being angry, Dad's voice had definitely been getting more worked up as he got to the end of that sentence. With "say", he'd thrown his hands in the air in despair, letting go of me for the first time. *Should I run away?* Then he grabbed my hand again.

'So . . .' Dad took a deep breath for himself. 'Are you going to calm down, so we can go and hear her out?'

*Ugh.* Did I really want to know what Darcie "wants to say"? It was just going to be all that stuff about Dadu again, wasn't it? But, I'd heard my parents talking as I sat on the stairs, Dad had said his decision was "final". Nothing Darcie could say would change that. But she was still going to try . . . *again* . . . trying to "fix" things.

I pressed my lips together. I didn't feel calm at all, but what else was I going to say?

'OK,' I said. 'I'm fine, we can go.'

Mum and Dad had arranged to meet at a pizza place down the road. Mum and the others had gone ahead, so we had a ten-minute, stonily silent walk for me to sort my head out. We weren't normally in town this late – a few people were wandering round in crazy high heels with loads of make-up and fancy clothes on. I blushed pink that I was holding my dad's hand like a little kid, but I didn't dare let go. Dad didn't seem to notice.

I snuck a glance at him. How much of the plan did he know? The France bit? Everything? I was going to be in so much trouble.

*Ugh, France.* Our storage trunk was still stashed by the bins, ready for its journey. And what about Ian? Would he remember my promise? Would he be waiting?

I imagined him, bags packed, little octopus suitcase at the ready, checking his octopus watch, shaking his head at his unreliable human friend. I sighed. Why not? That now seemed as believable as everything else I'd convinced myself of. How had I been so swept up in it? For weeks! I was starting to see my plan exactly as Darcie and Hassan must have seen it all along. If Darcie hadn't butted in and told me about the eggs, would I still be swept up in it now? *Right now.* Wheeling Ian away, headed for the train station?

'Come,' said Dad, tugging my hand but not looking at me. We crossed the road to avoid a huge group of people smoking outside a bar.

The warmth in my cheeks spread as far as my fingers and toes now. But the embarrassment wasn't from held hands this time, it was from how deeply I'd sunk into the whole plan – and, I had to admit, how horrible I'd been to my best friend. *Correction: ex-best friend.* As we walked, my anger melted away, leaving me hollow. I felt a bit bad I'd just hissed insults at her as she sat crying on the beach! Had I really thought I would set off to France by myself? I groaned.

Dad flicked a glance at me, and I tried to stifle it. But *towing an octopus through customs?* I'd slipped out of reality completely and into the world of my drawings. What else had I missed in the real world?

*Dadu.*

I knew it was true. That was who was waiting for me in the real world. I needed to face up to that and have the conversation with my parents I'd been avoiding. Confront Dadu's future. I couldn't let Darcie do it for me again.

'Are you ready for this, Sashi?' Dad made me jump. *Was he reading my thoughts?*

'Er . . . what?'

'I think you owe your friends an apology, don't you?'

I looked around blankly. We'd reached the pizza place. I peered through the window into a different world. Bathed in red light; warm and glowing and cosy. It couldn't be more different to the dark, cold street, where the sea wind was blowing white dregs of litter up and down. Something was thrown up against my foot and snagged there. I bent to pick it up – a cuttlefish bone, in the middle of town. I frowned down at it, then propped it against the wall like a totem.

Mum, Darcie and Hassan were gathered round a table, heads bent together, deep in an earnest looking conversation. I ached to join them, to be back where things made sense and I still had friends, but there was an impossible barrier between me and them. How could I go back after everything we'd done and said?

I pressed my fingers against the glass and Ian's face was suddenly in front of me. All the times I'd done that on Ian's tank and his suckered arms had risen to meet my fingers on the other side. Now no one on the other side of this glass even saw me. Tears welled in my eyes. *Could I do this?*

'C'mon, Sashi love. Through the door, not the window!'

Dad wrenched the door open. A wave of warmth hit me as he pulled me inside.

***

I took a deep breath and stumbled between the restaurant chairs, sucking in my stomach as I edged through tiny gaps mumbling 'excuse-me's.

**FACT: Octopuses have no bones, so can squeeze through spaces as small as their eyeball.**

Mum, Darcie and Hassan hadn't even noticed I was there but then, as I got closer, they all looked up at me.

'Hey,' I mumbled, with a shrug. *Apologise*. My voice froze in my throat.

'Come and sit down, my darling.' Mum pulled out the chair next to Darcie and I peered at it for a second before perching on the edge of the seat. Everyone already had drinks, and the table was covered with menus.

'This is for you.' Mum pushed a bottle of coke towards me, the paper straw already turning to mush inside.

'Thanks.' I held the bottle with both hands and sipped slowly. I didn't dare look around.

'What's everyone going to have?' Mum asked.

I risked a look up at Hassan. He was slouched in his chair, completely at ease, eyes scanning the options hungrily. How could he be so relaxed?

Dad leant forward over the table. 'Why don't you two girls *share* something, eh?'

My eyes flicked nervously to Darcie, seeing her face mirror my panic before we both looked away.

'Well!' Mum launched in, 'I'm sure everybody has their own choices. Have whatever you want girls. And you Hassan. Looks like they've got a vegan aubergine bake, so I'm sorted.' She was talking at double speed. 'Sashi are you going to have pepperoni again? You love that one.'

'Mmm . . .' Hassan finally looked up from the menu with satisfaction. 'I'm going for chilli squid. I've had it here before and its killer.'

Mum stopped talking and her mouth fell open a bit. 'Squid?' she said, after a pause. 'Don't you think . . . In the circumstances . . . Maybe . . .?'

I heard a snort to my left and looked to Darcie, whose hands had snapped to her face pointlessly, her laughter leaking round the sides.

Hassan turned to her, 'What?'

The pure innocence on his face set me off too, and I exchanged a look with Darcie before we both melted into the kind of giggles that were just uncontrollable vibrations.

'Hassan,' said Mum calmly. 'I think after tonight's octopus, er, *episode*, we should perhaps keep their cephalopod cousins *off* the menu, don't you?'

'Oh!' he said, realisation dawning. 'Ah man, what a shame, they're so delicious!'

That set me off again, tears streaming down my face. I turned to Darcie helplessly and her fingers found mine under the table.

'Hassan, you're the best,' she gasped out between giggles. 'How about the three of us just share a Margherita, eh?'

'Great,' said Mum, and managed to communicate it to the waiter in ten seconds flat.

'And the less said about tonight's "episode", the better,' chipped in Dad.

'I-told-you-I-wasn't-going-to-go-through-with-it!' I rushed out before he could shush me, but an icy glare warned me not to say anything else.

I felt a warm hand on my knee, as Mum turned back to the table. 'Actually, isn't that exactly what we're here to talk about, Manu?'

'Can we not just have some pizza firs—'

'We can eat and talk.' Mum meant business.

Turned out, Darcie had told them all about Project Free Ian this afternoon, including the France part, which she'd obviously learnt from Hassan, *and* her theory I'd been using Ian as a distraction from my "sadness about Dadu". I'd been amazed how quickly the conversation had moved passed my total idiocy and onto the topic of Dadu, but I'd already heard Dad's response to all that – his usual, "no".

'I know all this, Helen, we went over it this afternoon. I thought I'd made myself clear.' Dad was thinking the same as me: the Dadu topic was already closed. I rolled my bottom lip into my teeth and bit down hard, staring at the grease already gathering in pools on top of my pizza slice.

'Sashi?' enquired Dad. I blinked hard and forced myself to look up at him. 'Not visiting him . . . It isn't some sort of punishment, you know? Look, I know it's hard for you to understand, but I'm trying to protect you, not hurt you.'

'Dad, I don't need your protection from *Dadu*. I love him.'

'I know that, darling. I love him too . . . no . . . don't give me that look. He's my father and I love him. But he's not the same person any more—' I tried to protest, but he just shook his head and carried on.

'I know he's still in there, somewhere, but the

Dadu we interact with every day has changed; he's distant, he's confused, he can get angry. Listen, Sashi, it's not just that I don't want you to get hurt, I . . .' Dad's voice sounded thick, like he had something in his mouth. Was he going to cry? 'I don't want you to not *like* him any more; to stop loving him. Or to remember him like this, instead of how he was.' He drew himself up taller. 'You had a very special relationship, and that's how I want you to remember him.' He sniffed and tried to turn it into a laugh. 'OK?'

He said it like it was the end of the discussion.

'What do you mean "every day"?' I asked.

'Did you listen to anything I said, Sashi?'

I wiped my face, which was drenched with silent tears now, and did my own huge sniff. 'I heard you, Dad, but of course I wouldn't stop loving him. You have to have more faith in me. I understand what's happening to him, and . . . and that it's only going to get worse.'

I took a deep breath to steel myself. It was only as I'd said it out loud that I really understood for the first time. I wasn't going to make him better, or miraculously help him remember. The Dadu I'd grown up with really was gone.

But I still wanted to be there with him as he was now.

'I get it. But I'm not going to forget him, Dad.' I said it as firmly as he had, but as he opened his mouth to reply I rushed on. 'But you said you "interacted" with him "every day". I thought you weren't going to see him any more – same as me?'

'Er . . . yes.' Dad shifted uncomfortably, and in the side of my vision I could see Darcie and Hassan politely busy themselves eating.

'Look, I've been going every day, Sashi, sweetheart. I wasn't going to abandon him completely, of course not. But it's for me to deal with what comes next, not you – that's what being an adult is all about.'

'Mum's been going too.'

'Sashi!' Mum jolted, then settled back down, shrugging at Dad.

'Can we tell you about our new science project yet?' interrupted Hassan.

*What?*

'Yes,' said Mum.

Dad was turning from Mum to Hassan and back, his mouth opening and shutting, but Hassan just ploughed on before he could object. 'So, me and Darcie have been meeting up, right?'

*To laugh at me.* I hung my head, I couldn't look at either of them.

'And we've been doing loads of research into dementia.'

My head snapped up. Darcie's shrug was almost an apology, even after I'd shouted at her and told her to butt out of my life.

'Hang on a minute,' Dad interjected. 'This isn't really anything—'

'Manu, shush.'

'We found there's loads of research at the moment saying there are things you can do that might help people feel more in control and more comfortable. Y'know, calmer . . .'

Darcie beamed a look at me and it said, silently, "Is this too much? Or all OK?" I beamed one back, nodding, and it shouted, "It's wonderful, I'm so sorry. THANK YOU". She smiled.

Hassan was in the middle of an enthusiastic

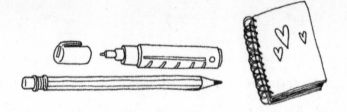

description. '. . . like, machines, that just play cool sounds. And there are kits where you can choose the smells you think he might like to remember best – gardens, or home cooking, or even boot polish . . . it's boss.'

*Dal*, I thought to myself, *Bubbling in the pan. That's the smell he would want.*

'Fake cats, to stroke. . .' Hassan was still going. 'I want one of those myself, to be honest.'

'But it's not all stuff you can buy,' Darcie picked up. 'Some of the research says it can just be sensory simulation that can help, like being stroked with a smooth cloth or having a jar of buttons to sort through. And a book of family memories to browse can be good . . . Hassan thought . . . well . . .' Darcie looked over at him.

'You should do him a comic, Sash! Of your family!'

I looked at Dad, who was sitting with both hands flat on the table in front of him, his face unreadable.

'The care home doesn't have the staff to experiment with all these things, Manu, but we could try,' suggested Mum quietly.

'Dad, I know he's not gonna go back to the way he used to be, or recognise me or anything.' I bit the inside of my cheek. 'I think maybe I did believe that before, but I get it now. And this . . . this sounds great!' I looked at my friends, full of love. I couldn't believe they'd been secretly researching this, while I was on my mad campaign. 'If we can make him more comfortable?'

Dad tipped his head on one side and reached a hand up and stroked my cheek. A tear on his own.

'What a grown-up girl you are, Sashi. And what good friends you've got.' *Yes.* Dad drew in a deep shaky breath and then let it out. 'OK, OK,' he said, and I felt Mum's hand on my knee again as Darcie made a "*squee*" sound. 'Let's try it, shall we?' he said. 'But Sashi, you must promise me to remember your wonderful Dadu as he was when he could remember every single thing about you.'

'I could never forget! And I'll draw a whole comic of it!'

# CHAPTER 24

'Don't expect miracles, Sashi, OK?' Mum tipped her head close to mine, talking quietly as the carer-lady rifled through an endless mound of paperwork behind the reception desk. 'The important thing is just to be present and if you feel uncomfortable, it's 100% OK to step outside and come back later. Or another day, even.'

'We promise we won't stop the visits this time, my love,' Dad chipped in, 'whatever happens.'

I opened my mouth to respond, but we were beckoned to follow by Dadu's carer, and suddenly we were moving.

I hugged the sketchbook and rummage box tight. I'd chosen the rummage box idea from Hassan and Darcie's list of suggestions and put it together myself. Just bits from his old house; fiddly things, textured things, interesting bits and bobs. I'd put in the wooden peacocks Dadu had had since he was a child.

And Dad's garage hoard had come into its own – it was like one giant, room-sized rummage box, after all!

Me, Mum and Dad had to scuttle to catch up as we were led down the corridors.

'We got your message, Mr Dutta, so he's in his room waiting for you. Although I'm not sure he'll thank you! All our residents normally join in the new music class on a Saturday morning now and he likes that one, you know. He always sits very calmly and happily. Into his music, was he, Mr Dutta Senior?'

'Oh. Er, no, not really.' Dad looked flustered.

Me and Mum exchanged a look, and she squeezed my shoulder. Music classes had been on Darcie and Hassan's long list of therapies. We'd been going to ask, but it seemed the home already did them. I wondered what else they did. Maybe he already had a rummage box? I tried to tell myself that would be a good thing not a bad thing.

'We'll come later then, next week,' Dad said. 'Could I get a list of class times from you and I'll be sure to avoid them if he enjoys them.'

'Of course you can, just pop by reception on your way out and I'll write them all down for you, not a problem. Although that's the one for him really. The others need a little more involvement, which I think is a bit beyond him right now – but he's always welcome to come along, of course.' The carer was talking into the air in front of her as she walked quickly ahead of us. She was quite short and old, and her legs were moving really fast. 'And you can come by and join in if you like.'

'Could we all come to the music class today?' I asked.

'Sashi!' Dad turned and glared at me, but wasn't this the point? That we were going to start trying these things.

The carer stopped in her tracks and turned to gawp at me. 'Well, it might be a bit of a squash, but I don't see why not, young lady. If your parents say it's OK . . .' she passed an appraising glance over Mum and Dad, then carried on walking. '. . . just wheel him along. Music room is just off the main sitting room on the right. Class starts in—' she checked her watch, '—twenty minutes!'

Mum widened her eyes at me, and I shrugged. We all followed the carer towards Dadu's room.

'It'll be better than staring at him, wishing he remembered!' I whispered to Mum. 'It'll keep us busy.'

'I guess so,' she whispered back, and smiled.

Then the carer opened the door to Dadu's room and all my hopes of keeping it together crumpled, along with me. Mum caught me as I fell into her, a sob erupting out of me before I had a chance to stuff my sleeve in my mouth and bite down on it.

He looked so small.

That was the main thing really. How had he shrunk in such a short space of time? He was thin and fragile looking. He used to be rounded and jolly like Dad, now he looked like you could snap him in two. And his once thick black hair was now just a few thin wisps of grey, standing high off his scalp. His cheeks were grey too, not their usual glossy brown.

I chewed on the fabric of my sleeve, feeling the texture of the fluff in my mouth. Mum's arms were warm around me as she gradually tilted me back on to my feet. She squeezed.

'All that time!' I turned to her. 'I should have been here instead of in the stupid aquarium! I should have realised.'

Mum pulled me into a hug. 'We all need to find our own way to process things, my love, it's the most natural thing in the world.'

'I needed time too, Sashi, remember?' Dad's face was folded in sadness. 'And Ian helped you work through your feelings. That was important. It's all OK.'

Dad kissed the top of my head and joined the carer, busying themselves around Dadu. The nurse left and Dad talked to Dadu cheerily, taking his hand. I wanted to hold his hand too.

I walked forwards.

'Hi, Dadu, it's Sashi.' I tried to look him in the eye, but his gaze slipped across me like I was a ghost and fixed on the door.

'I'm sure that woman said I should be expecting special visitors today,' he said vaguely. 'I really don't know who would be visiting me, but I have my music on a Saturday, and I don't want to miss it.' He padded his hands from side to side on the handles of his wheelchair as though he were trying to push himself to his feet. He was starting to look agitated.

'It's me Baba, it's Manu.' Dad tried to take his hand again, but Dadu was getting quite flustered now.

'I don't mean to be rude, but I really *am* expecting visitors, so if you don't mind . . .'

I turned to Mum in panic.

'We're here to take you to your class, Mr Dutta, don't worry.' *Why did she call him that? She never called him that.*

'Oh, to the music one?' He settled back down in his seat and his body seemed to ease. *OK, so that worked.*

'Yes, that's right. This young lady here is going to sit with you today. If that's OK?' *Me? I see.*

Dadu looked at me properly for the first time, his eyes running over my face, and smiled. My breath caught in my throat.

'Yes,' he nodded thoughtfully, 'that would be lovely. She looks like a very nice young girl.'

My eyes brimmed with tears, and I bit down on a sob.

'Do . . . do you mind if I take your hand, er . . . Mr Dutta?' I asked. Mum patted my back.

'Why not? Why not,' he said. When I took it, it felt just like his hand should. Thinner maybe, and you could feel the tendons on the back so clearly. And it looked wrong somehow, so pale. I stared at it for a second before I realised his thumb and finger were missing that faint yellow turmeric stain. But it was his all the same. I couldn't hold the sobs in any more, and he reached up and wiped the tears from my cheek with his other hand.

'Don't cry, little girl.'

'I knew this would be too upsetting,' said Dad's voice behind me.

I turned to him, wiping my tears on my shoulder. 'It's OK, Dad, honestly,' I whispered. 'I would rather be upset here, with him, than upset at home by myself.'

I held Dadu's hand all the way to the music room as Dad pushed, then all through the songs and then into the sitting room at Dadu's request, where we showed him the rummage box and comic.

'She's good with him, isn't she?' The carer had appeared behind us. We were all sitting, staring hopefully at Dadu while he browsed my drawings with a huge beaming smile on his face, saying nothing. It was the same smile he'd always had when looking at my pictures.

'What?' Dad turned reluctantly away. 'Who, Sashi?'

'Yes, this young thing. I've never seen him so calm. She can come any time she likes!' The carer carried on putting away the books that were piled up on the table behind us.

We turned back hopefully to Dadu – maybe just the tiniest flicker of a memory isn't too much to ask for? But I knew the answer before it happened. He closed the comic without a word and put it down next to him, picking up the rummage box again. He fished out a peacock and sat stroking his thumb back and forth down its back, telling us a story about someone. I wasn't sure if it was someone else from the home, or someone from his past.

Mum squeezed my shoulders. 'No miracles, remember?' She tucked a finger under my chin and made me look at her. 'Did you see his smile? That's the point. Something in those pictures made him deeply happy, even if he's not quite sure what, and that's a wonderful thing you did for him, isn't it?'

'Uh-huh,' I nodded. I tried to hold in the disappointment welling up inside me. No miracles. And she was right, that smile had been something special.

'I'm afraid it's time for us to go,' said Dad.

'Ha! Those visitors never turned up, did they?' said Dadu, and Mum squeezed my hand.

'Mr Dutta! These *were* your visitors – your family came to see you!' The carer spoke so briskly he seemed a little stunned, but then he ignored her completely. 'Are you ready to go back to your room now? Do you want to say goodbye to your visitors, and I'll take you back? Oh!' she turned to us then. 'You should all come along on our little trip next Sunday, if you fancy it? Your . . . "Dadu" is it? He inspired it, after all.' She reached out and patted me on the arm. 'We're all off to the aquarium!'

'The *aquarium*?' I couldn't hide my disbelief. Of all the places!

'All he goes on about, isn't it? Now, he *really* loves his fish, doesn't he? Have a tank at home, did he? One of those tropical ones?'

Mum and Dad exchanged a look. If they'd looked surprised at the music suggestion, they now looked completely thunderstruck.

'"Little fish" this, "little fish" that. Even in his sleep we've heard him say it. Day and night . . . "Little fish, little fish, little fish". Oh, he loves his little fish.'

Dadu frowned at her as she said it and then, for a second, turned and caught my eye.

'Little fish,' he said with a smile, and his eyes glistened with tears.

I felt each of my hands being scooped up by Mum and Dad and they squeezed.

# CHAPTER 25

'I know you're in there somewhere,' I said. 'Are you sulking at me? I mean, I get it if you are.'

I stared into the murky depths of Ian's tank, but I couldn't make out a single sucker. Not so much as the edge of a goose-bumped, camouflaged, colour-changing arm.

'We need to sort this out before tomorrow, Ian, because my Dadu's coming and I want to show you off to him. We have to make friends!'

Where was he?

*He can't really be sulking, because he's not really psychic, and we didn't really make a plan together.*

I had to remind myself of this fact.

FACT: Octopuses can use tools, show signs of individual personalities and even think with their arms, but there is NO evidence they're telepathic.

I mean, I knew it to be true now. I got it. I'd just believed it for so long, it was kinda hard to shake. Like, I don't really believe something terrible is going to happen when I see a single magpie, but I still feel the need to salute it. And now, I still wanted to apologise to Ian. If he would only come out! Maybe he was napping? Do octopuses have naps? Darcie would probably know. For all of my obsession, she'd learnt a lot more about octopuses than I had.

*Which reminded me.* There was another reason I'd come to the aquarium today. *Deep breath.* I had to go and see Martha; Darcie's favourite super-nice aquarium helper. I'd come back to Ian after his nap.

I asked around and eventually tracked down Martha at the gift shop. I was prepped and ready for a frosty reception; I'd been pretty unfriendly to her, after all.

'Hey! Tank-smasher! Good to see you!' she plonked down a huge crate of unsorted fish-themed toys and rushed over to give me a big hug.

So, not frosty.

'Where are the other terrible two? I've not seen them in ages! Is Hassan still planning to blow up my tunnel?'

'Oh . . . ha, ha, HA!' My fake laugh was the worst ever.

'Gosh! Sa— Oh, I'm so sorry, we only met the once and I've forgotten your name.' She looked mortified, hand to forehead. Hassan and Darcie had been back to see her multiple times, but I'd always avoided her – there was no way she should feel bad.

'Sashi,' I mumbled.

'Sashi-the-smashy!' She grinned. 'How could I forget? Well, Sashi, you're making me think Hassan seriously intended to do it!' Now she laughed.

'Er . . . Can I actually talk to you about something?' I asked. 'Somewhere private?'

She took me to the staffroom – the lion's den – and I risked telling her all about the plan I'd had, and, crucially, how Darcie and Hassan had stopped me. I told her I should have listened more to her expert info. She was pretty stern about my choices, but I moved it on to how much she'd inspired them both and how into sea life Hassan was, and science Darcie was. This was my plan – we all had to set up work experience placements for next year, and I knew placements at the aquarium were only available for GCSE kids generally, and even then like gold dust. I thought maybe . . . if I could wangle it . . . as a thank you . . .

'Of course!' said Martha. 'I can't think of two students better suited to help out here, they'd be wonderful.'

Heat flooded through me. I grabbed my phone out my bag, I had to tell Darcie straight away. But Martha laid her hand over the screen.

'Tell you what,' she said. 'Let's tell them tonight.'

'Tonight?' My hands flopped back down to my lap as I frowned up at her.

'Ask your parents if you can come back here at 8 p.m. I'll give you all a special night tour of the aquarium. There's something I'd like to show you.'

I swung by Ian's tank on the way out, expecting him to still be sulking, but there he was, in full splendour, gliding about, fully stretched-out and being admired by a group of young children.

I stood at the back of the pack and listened to them "ooh-ing" and "aah-ing" at him.

'Look at his eyes,' said one of them to his mum. 'He looked right at me! He's scary!'

I waited until the kids moved on then bent close to the glass. 'Soz, Ian,' I whispered. 'I know you want out of here, but there's nothing I can do.'

★★★

We arrived at the aquarium at 8pm on the dot. Mum and Dad had volunteered to escort us all: official parents-in-chief of the whole disastrous octopus project. Hassan's parents and Darcie's mum probably wouldn't have come anyway, but Mum and Dad would *not* want to risk them finding out what we'd been up to. Dad had already had a "man-to-man" chat with Hassan about keeping our "little adventure" secret. *So embarrassing.* They must be so ashamed of me.

'We're so proud of you, Sashi.' Mum reached out and laid a hand on my back.

My jaw dropped.

'They always wanted a criminal in the family,' giggled Darcie, scooping up my arm.

Mum sighed and smiled at Darcie with that weary, patient look she gets. It was weird to see it aimed at someone else. 'No, Darcie. I mean it. It took a lot of courage for Sashi to tell the aquarium staff the truth. I'm not sure *I* could have done it.'

Darcie looked sheepish. 'No, me neither.'

'That's the trouble with being good at everything, Darcie,' Dad chuckled. 'You don't get any practice at being wrong!'

278

'Dad!' Darcie didn't need practice at being wrong – she never was!

We were all huddled next to a huge canvas advert that was flapping noisily in the wind, its cartoon pirate and mermaid shivering.

'I-ripped-up-all-Sashi's-pictures!' Darcie flushed bright pink as she blurted it out. Mum actually gasped.

'But . . .' I stuttered. *She'd been right and I'd been wrong, surely? Like always.*

'I shouldn't have done that. It was horrible. I completely lost my temper.' She turned to me. 'I'm really sorry, Sash-a-lac.'

*Wow.*

I thought of the spirals of white paper drifting down to my bed, all my drawings destroyed, how heartbroken I'd been. Maybe she wasn't always perfect after all?

I squeezed her arm. 'It's OK.' *It was.*

We all stood in silence for a minute. I was happier than I'd felt in as long as I could remember.

'Hey, we should see if our escape pod is still there!' said Hassan, his eyes twinkling.

'Escape pod?' Darcie twisted her hair in gloved hands. 'What are you on about?'

'The storage trunk?' I asked.

'Well, if you want to be dull about it, I *guess*!' he laughed.

'It's what we were going to put Ian in,' I whispered to Darcie, tugging us all away from Mum and Dad to edge round the building. 'It should still be behind the bins.'

'You were so into the whole plan,' Darcie poked Hassan, 'admit it! I bet you were mad disappointed not to do it!' Her laugh rang into the night and Hassan guffawed along, as a huge gust of wind messed up his hair.

'Yeah, a bit. I wouldn't have done it, obviously. It was fun to plan, though. You were good at planning it, Sashi.'

'Oh, er, thanks?' I shrugged, then reached up and smoothed his hair back down. *That's better.*

'I told Matteo all about the whole thing,' he whispered. Me and Darcie gasped as one, but Hassan shrugged. 'He thinks you two are well cool.'

Darcie wrapped her arm round me, and we

swayed from side to side to keep warm until we nearly over-balanced, squealing.

'Yeah, look at us!' I giggled.

'If you play your cards right, we'll let you both sit with us at lunch!' Darcie winked at Hassan, but he just did his serious nod thing.

'That would be ace,' he said sincerely, stuffing his hands in his pockets and shuffling from foot to foot. 'Anyway, what's this night thing all about?'

'Guess we're about to find out!' Darcie pointed over my shoulder. 'Here's Martha!'

\*\*\*

'Sorry, sorry, sorry!'

Martha ran up, jangling a huge bunch of keys. She looked different in her home clothes; her hair was bouncing corkscrews round her face instead of scraped back in a pony.

'The bus took for ever. OK, are you guys ready?' She grinned at us, and we nodded back like eager puppies. She turned to Mum and Dad, hand out for a shake. 'Hi, I'm Martha Thacket, Deputy Head of Research at the aquarium.'

*Oh. Didn't know that.*

Mum and Dad said all the usual grown-up stuff, then Martha turned about three different keys in three different locks, THEN put the key code in the keypad.

*Keys.*

Me, Darcie and Hassan all looked at each other, then bent double laughing.

'What's got into you lot?' asked Mum.

'It's . . . it's OK,' said Darcie. 'It's just, maybe, the whole . . . y'know . . . thing we were worried about . . . might not have got very far after all.'

We wouldn't have even got past the front door! Mum just frowned and we all followed Martha into the dark building.

'Oh,' said Martha. 'I nearly forgot.' She turned on a light. 'Sashi, do you want to tell your friends your surprise before we get started?'

Everyone turned to look at me and I blushed.

'Oh, OK, well, I've not been a great friend to either of you recently. I asked you to do something . . . well . . . *illegal* with me.' I caught the silver flash of a passing fish in the corner of my eye. Surreal. 'I lied to you. I got jealous, and mad when you didn't want to go along with the plan with me, Darcie, and, no, no, listen . . .'

She was shaking her head and trying to grab my shoulders in a hug. But I held her hands, so she had to be still for a second.

'. . . even more mad when you tried to tell me the truth about what was going on. All this time, you've stuck by me and been the best friend I could ever imagine, despite me being a total cow.'

'It was all my fault, Sashi. I encouraged you. I thought I knew what was best.' She was still shaking her head. 'I should have talk—'

'Shh! All the dementia research and stuff. It's amazing.'

'And *I* was a total cow to Hassan, remember?'

'Yeah, that's true.' Hassan shrugged but looked strangely happy with the fact.

'Stop! You're ruining my apology! *Anyway*, I can't make it up to you. But Martha can!'

*That* shut them up. They both turned to her with looks of total confusion, and she handed them each a piece of paper.

'My boss made it official this afternoon. She's waived the age restriction of work experience placements here for you two, so if you want them, next term's placements are yours.'

Darcie clapped her gloved hands together, then she hugged me, then Martha.

Hassan was nodding with a lopsided smile. 'That is totally dope, I would love that.'

Mum squeezed my shoulder.

'It's not enough,' I said, putting my arms around my friends, 'but I wanted to say thank you.'

'It's fabulous!' Darcie gave me a big wet kiss on my cheek.

'Ugh, Darce!' I laughed, wiping it off.

'Right!' said Martha, clapping her hands as if we were a school tour. 'Who wants to come and see . . . Ian, isn't it?'

We trooped round to his tank – Darcie clutching the placement info to her chest – but Ian couldn't be seen. I hid the tiniest wave of disappointment.

Nothing was going to dim my glow now Darcie and Hassan were happy with the placements, but I didn't really get the night tour thing. I'd kinda assumed maybe Ian would be more active at night or something.

But no, he was just hiding again.

'Can anyone see him?' asked Martha.

We all craned our necks, going low and high . . . but, nothing.

'He was doing this this morning,' I said. 'He's just hiding.'

'Well, not exactly . . .' said Martha.

'The camouflage must be amazing.' Mum's nose was touching the glass.

'. . . he's not there.' Martha finished.

*What?*

''Well, where is he then?' Dad sounded a little impatient. Like when he got mad in restaurants and asked for his money back.

'I'll tell you a good fact about octopuses,' said Martha. 'Did you know, they can fit through any space bigger than their eyeballs?'

'Whaaat?' Hassan's jaw looked like it might disconnect.

I knew it already though. It was a pretty beginner-level octo-fact.

Martha was pointing to something at the top of Ian's tank. 'See those tubes up there? That's where we drop his food in – they actually have a larger diameter than his eyes.'

But those tubes were *tiny*. What was she saying? That he could . . .?

'Where do they lead?' asked Darcie. 'Is he OK? Doesn't he need water?' She sounded a little panicked.

*Huh? Oh!*

My heart started beating faster. Had Ian got out of his own tank?

'Wow,' said Mum.

'Actually,' said Martha, 'your octopus friend has been escaping from his tank most nights since he was first brought here. We discovered it when a few of the smaller crabs started going missing from the rock-pool exhibition.' I exchanged a look with Hassan. Snacks. 'He clearly thought we weren't providing interesting enough food,' Martha continued. 'Now we leave him trays of specially prepared nibbles in hard-to-reach places, as little challenges, to keep his life interesting.'

'You know, I've read about this kind of thing.' My Dad had his hands on his hips and was shaking his head. 'How do the newspapers not know about this?'

'Well, we do prefer to keep it within the aquarium,

Sir. I hope you understand. We're still researching his behaviour and we don't want a frenzy.'

'Most aquariums clamp the lids on octopus tanks shut, to stop them sneaking out. But we didn't want to limit . . . er, Ian's . . . adventures. And we've learnt a lot more about him.'

She turned to me. 'Now, what I thought you in particular might be interested in, Sashi, is that every morning, when we come to re-open the aquarium, where do you think we find him?'

I looked into Martha's kind brown eyes and realised why she'd brought us here. I turned to Darcie and Hassan, as the realisation sank into all of us like a tidal wave of relief, responsibility lifting.

'Right back in his tank,' I said.

# EPILOGUE

### ... THE NEXT DAY

I sat down on the too-small chair with a satisfied sigh and rested my forearm on the colouring-in table. This was going well. The lights flashed from blue to red to green and reflected from Dadu's thin face as he looked around with awe from his wheelchair. We'd been in nearly every room now, and Dadu had been engrossed with all of it. But I was saving the best till last.

He craned around behind him so I turned us both so he could see the snake-necked turtles diving gracefully amongst the tropical fish. I took his hand and stroked the paper-thin skin as he watched them silently, a quiet smile on his face.

'Thank you,' he said, and drew my hand on to his lap, patting it with his other hand, 'my little fish.'

I gasped.

'See!' The carer from last week was passing at just that moment, holding an old lady up by the elbow. The lady was walking in small, determined steps on tree-trunk ankles towards the Rainforest Zone. 'Told you! Loves them, he does!' They kept going and I stood up and kissed my dadu on the top of his head. It was more than I'd dreamt of, and it was enough.

'C'mon, Dadu, I want you to meet someone special.'

Dadu looked at me blankly then, eyes glazed with confusion, and I knew he had no idea who I was again. But it didn't matter.

'You'll like this one, Mr Dutta,' I said.

He settled back in his chair, and I pushed him to Ian's tank until his face was up to the glass. Ian swooshed out. Grey to brown to rusty red to orange. Arms swirling and scrolling, his body moving like ocean currents side to side across the tank.

'This is Ian the Octopus,' I said. 'Supreme cephalopod intelligence and escape artiste extraordinaire.' As I spoke, Ian shifted so his bulging eyes lifted above his long suckered arms and Dadu moved his face even closer to the glass. Their two sets of eyes reflected each other's.

'So, I used to think Ian wanted to escape to the ocean to be with his family,' I told Dadu, 'but turns out he's doing OK where he is, being looked after by professionals who know what's best for him. So long as people visit him every now and again.' My hand was resting on Dadu's shoulder. '. . . and he had plenty of crabs to eat.'

Dadu lifted his fingers to the glass and Ian slowly raised a suckered arm to meet them. Neither of them moved as Ian hung there in the water. The hair on the back of my neck prickled as I watched him stare into my Dadu's beloved eyes.

Who knows what they said to each other.

THE END

# ACKNOWLEDGEMENTS

First of all, thank you to my utterly wonderful daughters Alma and Ada.

Alma: always my first reader — really deserves a writing credit, as most of my best ideas are actually hers. Always there to remind me to add an animal and share her thoughtful critiques. Ada: who was 6 months old when I decided to take this writing thing seriously, and is now (nearly) old enough to read this book herself — seeing her start on a proof copy the minute it came through the door filled me with joy.

Girls, you inspire the best bits in every character I write. All the kindness, creativity, boldness and mischief comes from you! But you're both a million times more interesting and delightful than any character I could invent. You make my days magic and my love for you both is endless.

Thank you, too, to the rest of my pack of wonderful kid readers, who correct my slang, amaze me with their insight and provide boundless (emoji) encouragement; my nephews and niece, Ollie, Arlo, Joe and Lucy, as well as the lovely Vaari, who is an insightful and only slightly brutal critic.

Thank you to my other early readers. Jen — I braced myself for your opinion and still don't actually believe you like it, of course. You are my anchor, and the only person I trust to be as brutal and honest as myself. Super special thanks to my sensitivity readers, Heena and Jess. It was a big ask and you both did it with such diplomacy, honesty and grace, contributing so much and helping me see Sashi's world more clearly. I'm endlessly grateful for the changes you helped me to make, they're among my favourite moments of the book. Heena, I feel like I've been pestering you for years now, I promise to stop! Thanks to Ash too, for your cultural pointers and helping me settle on the name Dadu (and your voice notes on how to pronounce it!). And also to your papa, Mahesh, for allowing me to share his image with Selom and Lucy. Caswell — I didn't rely on you for animal facts this time, so I'm thanking you in advance for not correcting the ones I did use! Claire and David — I gave you the wrong book to read, this one is literally half the length. Sorry about that.

To my writing friends, who understand everything. My critique partner and fount of all wisdom Oliva Shaw. Carey Camburn — and all the other writers in my Clifftop Crew — seeing your creativity up close always leaves me in awe and pushes me to try harder in my own writing. Lindsey Galvin, for your time and kindness, and for not being too put out that I had also — co-incidentally — written a book about a girl who likes to draw the octopus in the Brighton Aquarium! To the 2022 debut group who let me sneak in to gather their wisdom, experience and support, and the 2023 debuts — I can't wait to see what this year holds for us all and read every one of your books!

My real life friends, you know who you are, thank you. Becky, I'm holding you to your promise — a gift for every child you know!

There are so many lovely, talented people who worked on this book — the collaboration has been a joy.

My amazing agent Emily, I trust your insight and instinct and am sooo glad you're prepared to share it with me with no fuss. Thank you for killing off the various ridiculous sub-plots I originally planned to scatter all over this book and re-focus me on the relationships. Your editing is everything. Molly, thank you for stepping in and taking me to the finish line. My editor Kathy, thank you for seeing through my fudges. I apologise for my terrible spelling. Selom: you were top of my cover artist wish-list. I'm still in shock you actually did my cover! And it's beautiful! Lucy: the book's super talented illustrator/ comic artist/ life-giver, your illustrations made me cry, thank you. All at UCLan: Charlotte, Graeme, the very talented Amy and publishing powerhouse Hazel; whatever this is, it is all down to you. Thank you for loving Sashi, Dadu, Ian and taking a risk to share their story with the world.

Special thanks to Mal, aka Skeleton Jones, for the concept art that originally brought Sashi and Ian to life. I love your art and I'm still amazed and grateful that you donated your time and talent to help get this book off the ground. For inspiration, I owe a lot to Peter Godfrey-Smith's amazing book Other Minds, as well as the street artists of Brighton.

So much of my own childhood is in this book, so I owe thanks to my own grandparents, Nanny Erdington and Nanny London, and to Hank. My snatches of childhood memories have helped me jigsaw together a picture of love, happiness and grandparental kindness.

Thank you Monica, for so many things, but in this context specifically for the drawer of paper dolls at your house when we were growing up, that morphed here into Dadu's drawer of stationery. For the beautiful, tactile eggs that became Dadu's peacocks.

To my parents-in-law, Tara and Pete, who despite years of my hiding away to 'write' never once suggested I might want to get a proper job. I'm so pleased my girls get to experience that precious grandparent relationship with you both.

Jimmy. My number one supporter in all things, who is a constant source of inspiration and encouragement for all creative endeavours. And indeed life endeavours. And everything. And for, y'know, the bins.

And to my Mum, the root of any imagination and empathy I may have used to write this. So much of Dadu's warmth and creativity came from what you were like as a Mum, then as a Nanny and Nana to your grandchildren, especially in those two precious years with Alma. I wish I could thank you properly.

# HAVE YOU EVER WONDERED
# HOW BOOKS ARE MADE?

UCLan Publishing is an award winning independent publisher specialising in Children's and Young Adult books. Based at The University of Central Lancashire, this Preston-based publisher teaches MA Publishing students how to become industry professionals using the content and resources from its business; students are included at every stage of the publishing process and credited for the work that they contribute.

The business doesn't just help publishing students though. UCLan Publishing has supported the employability and real-life work skills for the University's Illustration, Acting, Translation, Animation, Photography, Film & TV students and many more. This is the beauty of books and stories; they fuel many other creative industries! The MA Publishing students are able to get involved from day one with the business and they acquire a behind the scenes experience of what it is like to work for a such a reputable independent.

The MA course was awarded a Times Higher Award (2018) for Innovation in the Arts and the business, UCLan Publishing, was awarded Best Newcomer at the Independent Publishing Guild (2019) for the ethos of teaching publishing using a commercial publishing house. As the business continues to grow, so too does the student experience upon entering this dynamic Masters course.

www.uclanpublishing.com
www.uclanpublishing.com/courses/
uclanpublishing@uclan.ac.uk